LIKING GOOD JAZZ

BY THE SAME AUTHOR

Timberdick's First Case

MALCOLM NOBLE

Liking Good Jazz

Matador
9 De Montfort Mews
Leicester LE1 7FW, UK
Tel: 0116 255 9312
Email: matador@troubador.co.uk
Web: www.troubador.co.uk/matador

ISBN 1 904744 96 6

Cover illustration: © Photos.com

This is a work of fiction. All characters, locations and events are imaginary,
and any resemblance to actual persons, locations and events is purely coincidental.

Typeset in 10.5pt Stempel Garamond by Troubador Publishing Ltd, Leicester, UK
Printed and bound by The Cromwell Press Ltd, Trowbridge, Wilts

Matador is an imprint of Troubador Publishing

PART ONE

MONDAY, TUESDAY AND WEDNESDAY

ONE

The Top of Old Moore's Lane

The racing was over, the dogs had gone home and dumpy Mo Tucker, the lavatory cleaner, waddled up Old Moore's Lane. She didn't like doing it at night because Old Moore's was a dark alley without lamps, but the stadium gates had already been shackled and Mo was determined not to spend another night locked in. So, she squashed herself through the chain link fence and started – slowly, uncomfortably – to toil up the hill. She knew it would make her sweat. All her life, she had been wanting not to.

Race cards, spent slips and fag butts littered the way. The crowd had trudged along the alley two hours before and Mo fancied that she could taste the ale on their breath. The paving stones still echoed with their banter. Bubble and chunter, Mo called it. The old men had been sure that something was queer about the card but they knew that their tussle with the racing managers was a good piece of the sport. And hadn't it been a privilege – 'a privilege, I mean!' – to see Wen's Flower leap from the traps in Race Six? 'She'll come in for us next month in the semi's.' As the floodlights grew more distant, and the cold and misty evening chilled their sweat, the men had cursed the idea of wearing woollens under their old suit jackets. The women swore too – for there were as many women as men, some in groups of half a dozen, some with husbands and lovers, a few on their own. Tramping up Old Moore's Lane put everything out of joint. Bones, pride, temper and stitching. Mo had seen the fat women tugging at the straps beneath their armpits and the men stretching so that the whiskers on their throats came free of their collars. But they were all gone now. The old men and women, the teddy boys and scallywag girls. The dirt

3

from their soles was crisping on the stony ground.

She saw an empty wallet and purse in the gutter. She had heard that the pickpockets had done well; not one had his collar felt. And the Johnny machine in the Gents had been empty before nine. Mo guessed that a dozen girls might have been started tonight. In the old wooden sheds or up against the wall of the Steward's Lodge where it was too dark to get told off. Maybe, a couple of the girls had left early through Old Moore's Gate – that's what they called the hole in the fence – and had laboured up the hill, unsteady on their feet, already pregnant and wanting weak tea and a smoke in Jack's all-night caf.

Mo's walking was hard work too. The unsteady paving stones tilted this way and that, so that her waddling resembled the pitching of a creaky old dinghy in choppy waters. She was still in her twenties but her shape and dowdiness gave her extra years; she looked past it. Mo Tucker would be an easy woman to rob. Puffing and panting and grumbling out loud, she kept her eyes on the yellow light of the café. It was like a beacon guiding her in. Behind her, a slow goods train clattered across the viaduct. The first of the church clocks began its three quarter chime and Mo, in her silly way, counted in the other parts to a familiar symphony. St Faith's joined half way through and when both had finished the Abbey College was sounding like their echo on the edge of the city. Mo expected the Council House clock to start a full minute late. She thought, no time's right in this town; you take it as you like.

A provocatively dressed woman with a stick-like figure was leaning against the café's back drainpipe. A scrubber, Mo thought. She had bent one knee so that she could dig the heel of her shoe into the old cement between two bricks in the wall. She dug it in and twisted it; never mind how much it marked the plastic. The pose emphasised her dark nylons and white shoes and made sure that her mini-skirt grew short enough to show the tops of her stockings.

Mo stopped. She wanted to know what the tart was doing here. She'd get no business at the top of Moore's Lane. Perhaps she had agreed to meet someone? But why here? Why would she agree to meet someone in the alley? She'd get no other men if he didn't turn up.

"One who knows no better than she ought," Mo muttered as she stepped forward again. She recognised the old prostitute. Timberdick Woodcock had been working on the streets for almost twenty years. Most of the girls moved on after a year or two but some of the old stagers – girls like Timberdick and black Layna and old Slowly Barnes – still hung around, like remnants hanging from a rusty nail on a dirty brick wall. She was a lightweight woman with boyish hips and gangly limbs that might have looked cute, three years ago, but Timberdick was in her middle thirties now and beginning to look scrawny. Timbers wasn't good looking. Her legs were like matchsticks. She had no chin and her nose and eyes were too big for her face. But, in the last year, she had started to spend money on her hair (rather than trusting to friends) and she had learned to look forward to lunches and teas rather than snacks, giving her face a richer complexion. The extra care meant that she could have an attractive smile – if she bothered; Timberdick was still a girl who giggled stupidly and never smiled on purpose.

She saw Mo looking. "Mind your own business, you old cow," she said as the lav-lady approached.

'Old cow?' thought Mo. 'You could give me five years and I'd still be younger than you.' She said nothing.

A black cat, her tail up, crossed in front of her and Mo stopped and tugged at the collar of her blouse until she had recited a verse from the Bible backwards. Two days later, Mo told the policeman that the cat and the ritual had laid a curse on Old Moore's and everyone who was awake would be touched with wickedness. Black stardust, she called it. Mind, only Mo and the skinny tart were there to be damned. (The man came later when the cat and its black magic was way off.)

Keeping an eye on the petulant whore, Mo moved to the other side of the alley. Careful to say nothing. Careful not to look her directly in the face. Careful to hurry without running away. (Mo knew how to get out of the way of bullies.)

"What are you looking at then!"

She could have said, 'I was thinking that a man wouldn't have to try hard to catch a peep at your knicker stitching.' But she kept it all in her head.

Timbers wanted to pick a fight.

The bloke was twenty minutes late and probably wouldn't come at all now. Timberdick was irritable not merely because she had been let down – Lord, show her a working girl who hadn't wasted time in that way – but also because she was three quarters of a mile from her regular pitch – the little bit of pavement opposite the Hoboken Arms where men looked for their sparky bitch with spindly legs, a good bum and well-dressed breasts. Fiery and coarse and dirtier than she had ever been, that was Timberdick. But tonight, somebody-bloody-else would be taking her money. If the bloke turned up now – Lord, if he did – she'd charge him four or five times as much. Six times as much. And if he didn't? Well, Timbers was itching to scratch someone's eyes out.

When Mo walked into the empty café, Jack was on his feet and pouring hot tea from the big aluminium teapot. Usually, he spent his time in an armchair behind the counter, out of sight of customers, and played military music on a reel-to-reel tape recorder underneath.

He pushed her tea across the counter and said, "Leave her." Eight years of night work had taught him to be a man of few words.

"You ought to phone the p'lice. Cursing and swearing as she does."

"Ned'll sort it." He had already withdrawn to the armchair. He wiped the sweat from his neck with an old hand towel. "He'll be in after his refs."

Mo took her cup and saucer to a table by the door. She could see Timbers through the window. Her figure was so slight and bony that a man with a pen and ink could have caught her outline in just a couple of strokes. But the yellow light falling across her awkward face gave away much more. Pint-sized Timbers was in a strop.

"Are you goin' to call a taxi for me?" Mo pleaded.

Jack was working the tape recorder now. After an age, he said, "Dave'll run you home. He'll be in."

People called Timbers' punter 'The Man from Scurries' because he had worked at the gentleman's outfitters for thirty-one years. Longer than most people had lived in the city. Sometimes, he was simply 'Scurries' and that niggled him because it wasn't his habit to scurry anywhere. The nickname made him sound like a squirrel. Or a fat mouse.

He was forty-eight, neat and portly, so 'fat mouse' was a name that people might use, but he always dressed smart. He walked quickly, ate moderately (with thin lips, he liked to think) and drank only mild beer. His deafness let him down – it had been enough to keep him out of the army and it discouraged him from driving a car at night. There was only his deafness – and his big worry.

Timbers saw him coming and she groaned. She hated men with sticking-out stomachs, especially the fit ones. They hurt her. They always wanted to lift her on top of their bellies and pull her apart. He'd want to kiss her while her feet were off the ground. Well, she wasn't bloody doing it. She'd make it clear what he was paying for. And nothing else.

"You already owe me," she demanded. "You know that."

"You'll be well paid." He spoke like a shopkeeper who always knew better than his customers. Polite but patronising. 'A bloody undertaker,' she thought. 'That's what he's like. God, he'll be weird. He'll want me to do it like a done-up body.'

He adjusted his spectacles. "First, I want to be sure you understand the requirements."

"Oh, I understand," she said, giving him no room to build on his fantasy. "You want to do me in a railway carriage. Not much to say about that, is there? Twenty minutes, once we get there. That's all. You get it? And I hope you've got a bloody car. I'm not bloody walking to the station."

"The girls said you've entertained on trains before."

"They meant I got into trouble last year for shaking my bra at engine drivers. I hadn't got it on at the time. Truth was, I hadn't got much on at all."

"You'll play along with it, then? You'll fit in with my story."

"Look, I'm bloody frozen standing here and I'm not spending all night playing trains with a bloody schoolboy."

Scurries accepted jokes about grown-up schoolboys with their trains. To tell the truth, he was beginning to think that he had been a much better boy than he was a man. People had valued him during his childhood. They had praised his diligence and promised him a good future. These days, folk looked at him and saw the portly mouse that was second-in-charge of a tailor's shop and ridiculed by his family. He took out his wallet. "You will need a little extra because I'm late."

Looking through the misty window, Mo saw Timbers fold the

7

money into her bra and pull the woollen cardigan from behind the drainpipe. "We can't let her," she said, quietly at first, then more loudly and again until Jack asked what the matter was. "We can't let her go off with him. I've seen what he does."

Jack said nothing. Timbers was already trotting after the man.

"Jack!"

"Ned'll be in," he said without alarm. "He'll sort it out."

But Mo was sure that something bad was going to happen and she wanted to cry. Her face wobbled as she kept the tears in. "Ned listens," she mumbled incoherently. "Ned trusts me."

She stirred the spoon in the cup. Just think about your cup of tea, she told herself. (The doctor had told her that, whenever Mo wanted to cry, she should concentrate hard on something small.)

"Where's Ned?" she said. "He should be in by now."

The first spots of rain speckled the windowpane.

TWO

Last Train Home

The railway station was resting. Breathing out, Fred Leaper called it. The booking office and tearooms were locked, and empty carriages stood at three platforms like well-behaved children in lines. Midnight drizzle crept in from the platform ends and, high above, something discarded had caught in the steel girders and was making a noise like a bird with big wings flapping. The last man home was called the nightwatchman but old Fred Leaper wasn't going to stay all night. He meant to be on his way as soon as the 00:47 was safely in and bedded down. The driver and guard, unless they were local men, would sleep in the Ladies Waiting Room (the Ladies, because there was a coal stove, a warm thick carpet and properly upholstered armchairs) before catching an early morning train back to London. One of them would peg the nightwatchman's clock at two o'clock and the other at four. A young railway hand had already agreed to bring his early shift forward. So, Fred would work until one o'clock, be credited with a full nightshift and have the following day to himself. He would have been appalled by any suggestion that flexing the shift was a cheat. It was a fair system; the job got done and everyone had his turn. And Fred was a conscientious railwayman, proud of his employment and diligent. Although the Ladies Room was open and a supper had been left for him as well as the 00:47 men, Fred would never have been caught sitting down when he should have been on his feet. As he waited for the last-train-in, he patrolled, swinging an old fashioned Tilly lamp at his side. He checked the maintenance of the platforms, gates, lights, window catches and luggage trolleys. He carried a wad of small repair forms in his pocket so that he could initiate any requisition promptly. Like all railwaymen, he was proud of his station. He had been schooled at a small one-platform affair on the edge of the city and abided by the attention to detail that had been life itself to his first stationmaster. Always, he picked up litter when he found it.

Every now and then, his light would catch the tearoom's window and the face of a boy-child would appear like a ghost in the glass. The advertising poster should have been pasted over, years ago, but the lad had been chewing sweets for so long that his survival had taken on a superstition. The station staff protected his space and regulars had adopted his image as folklore. Only Fred properly understood how reflecting a lamp from the end of Platform Five could bring the boy's face to the restaurant window. Truthfully, the young railway hand was the only other one who wanted to understand. Fred stayed late one night to explain but wound up frustrated: something that was obvious to him proved too complicated for words. For the others, knowing what happened, but not knowing why, gave their favourite ghost an aura of harmless but true mystery.

Fred's ankles bothered him. They were always painful these days, red, peeling and ready to blister. They screamed with cold but an extra pair of socks would have chafed them badly. Fred Leaper's boots seemed much heavier than they used to be. He never mentioned it and, living alone, didn't need to.

When he reached the farthest end of the longest platform, he stood, his face wet with the weather, and looked into the night. He could see very little. Derelict carriages rested on the breakers line, two hundred yards from the main station. Their shabby paintwork and cracked woodwork, offensive to a railwayman like Fred, looked worse in the dark and wet. Further away, the Council House clock tower lifted itself above the mist like St Paul's in the smoke of an air raid and, because he knew where to look, he spotted the pinhead lights of the approaching train, five or six miles off. Opposite Fred's vantage point – the railway terminus was raised above the road – The Station Road Hotel was unusually quiet; just one or two lights burned in upstairs bedrooms. The drinkers had gone home long ago. The bus station was empty; the toilets were locked to keep the needies away. The hot dog man was packing up his stand beneath the railway bridge and, there-fore, almost under Fred's feet. A taxi was waiting in the bus bay. Perhaps the taxi was to take the hot dog man home, but the men weren't talking to each other. The pigeons were asleep, wherever they were. Cats kept out of sight. And no mongrel dogs prowled the narrow, broken pavements. Fred stood on the concrete peninsular and wondered if, anywhere in the world, anyone was talking to anyone tonight.

* * *

Timberdick and the man called Scurries hurried across the cinders like refugees in flight. His unbuttoned overcoat waved in the wind. He carried a small brown suitcase.

"Bloody wait," Timbers squawked. The portly man was dodging this way and that and going well. "Bloody didn't say I'd have to do this, did you?"

"It's not far." He had crossed four tracks and was running along the sleepers of the down-at-heel siding. The lights of the terminus were three hundred yards ahead and set above them like a theatre stage. When he spotted the swinging light from Fred's Tilly lamp, Scurries dipped his head but still made speed. A curious figure, like a fat puppy with paws on motors.

Timbers had trouble keeping up with him. Her sparrow's legs weren't made for running. Her ankles buckled on the cruel cinders and her arms and elbows stuck out like awkward levers.

"You never said this," she grumbled.

"I said in a railway carriage," he insisted shortly.

"You never said out here. Bloody railway carriage means a bloody station." And she cursed as she cut her foot another time.

Timbers stopped. "Listen."

"It's nothing," he said, knowing that she had detected the first clatterings of the last train. "It's miles off."

"Bloody better be," she said.

Lord, she hadn't stopped complaining since they got out of his car. Hadn't he paid her enough? Twice as much as she would have earned on the pavements of Goodladies Road. The truth was he would have preferred almost any other woman to Timberdick Woodcock. She was older than he pictured and she wasn't good looking.

But the others wouldn't agree to go with him, so far from their

11

beats for so long. 'You wanna talk t'Timbers," they said. 'She likes railway lines and dressin' up.' He knew that they were making fun of him. Anyone who got stuck with Timbers was a joke.

"Here." He had reached the broken railway carriages at last. Even he was surprised by how high above the ground they were, without a platform. "Here, you'll have to help me clamber up. Once I've got a door open, I can pull you in."

"What d'you mean? Help you clamber?" She stood with her hands on her hips, panting in the night. Almost out of patience, she couldn't understand what he wanted her to do. He was twice her weight. How was she supposed to help?

She made a back for him – bloody hell, the things a girl has to do – then suffered in silence as he trod on her and reached for the brass handle of the carriage door. She was sure that his boots had cut into her.

"Quiet," he hissed. They could hear other trespassers on the railway. Two hundred yards away, perhaps, on the other side of the tracks.

"Bugger 'quiet', pull me up." Timbers shivered with cold. She was wearing her flowing woollen sweater now. She looked all legs and knees as he pulled her up and through the carriage door. The cold had numbed her lips and turned her pasty face red. As she trod along the corridor of the carriage, her nose started to run. She wiped it on the sleeve of her cardi. "We'll bloody freeze," she grumbled. "Doing it here."

He wanted to say that she would be no colder here than coasting with a bloke on the pavements, but something more important was bothering him. "There'll be no lights," he said. He had counted on being able to see her, sitting in a corner seat, cool and unconcerned. That was part of the fantasy. For God's sake, a big part.

"We'll have to carry on," he said quietly.

"Not bloody taking my sweater off."

He opened the door of a First Class compartment and ushered little Timberdick inside. "We're here now," he said.

"We're here now," she mimicked. Like a schoolboy on bloody holiday, he was.

"Please, Timbs. Play along with it."

12

She looked him plain in the face. "How long have you been working this out?"

Scurries could not remember when he had first dreamed of sex in a train. The two notions became so coupled in his mind that he could not do one without thinking of the other. When he made love, he pictured trains. When he travelled by train, he dreamed of sex. But the dreams had never come true and now he was forty-eight and, recently, he had began to worry about the obsession. He needed to do it. So strong were his feelings that he had began to avoid railway journeys for fear that he might find himself alone with a woman passenger and he might misinterpret the opportunity. He had even put off business trips to London, at some cost to his reputation.

Last Christmas Day, he decided. He'd do it in the New Year. For real. He would plan it and arrange it and carry it out and, then, consider it done. Dead and buried in 1964. (The New Year, he said, but it took him eleven months to fix.) He started to take evening walks, looking at the places, the people, and the things that could get in his way. He soon discovered the disused carriages with easy access from the playing fields and, within a couple of weeks, had got to know the terminus staff. 'Gary' Cooper in charge, Meg in the tearoom, old Fred Leaper and George Croak (they didn't get on), and the lad from the Stretton flats. They didn't worry that he was spending time with them; so many enthusiasts liked to sit with railwaymen and talk over mugs of tea. Scurries carefully assembled intelligence about their night work and worked out a plan. At half past twelve he and the girl would climb the sportsfield fence and run along the dark embankment to the old railway carriages. They would wait in a First Class compartment and he would time their liaison just as the 00:47 rumbled into the station. He ran the pictures through his mind, night after night.

But he needed an obliging woman. Old Shiel would have done it if he had asked, but he realised that sex in a train means sex with a stranger, so his wife wouldn't do. A friend or neighbour might have satisfied the role and he did spend weeks considering first one woman then another, but he saw no-one he could trust. So he started to ask the girls who stood on the street corners and alleyway pavements of Goodladies Road. This presented an opportunity to choose a girl who best matched the images that had dogged his sleep for years.

Mid thirties. Dark hair. Comfortable to sit in the corner of a railway carriage with her legs tucked beneath her as she read a magazine, touching her hair every now and then, knowing that he was watching her and not minding it. But the girls turned him down. Not just the first and second girls but every one that he approached. They passed him from one to the other, not because another was likely to agree but because every girl deserved the opportunity to giggle at this bloke with the weird idea. Scurries tried to be patient – he understood what was going on – but as weeks turned into months, his frustration grew. Having taken the decision to bring his fantasy to life (and, God knows, wasn't he risking enough?) and having carefully planned the affair, he was being thwarted by the fickleness of females. He had agreed to pay them fairly, hadn't he? They made themselves available to others, didn't they?

The girls knew that the job would end up with Timberdick.

She sat in the corner seat, with her knees up to her chin and her bony fingers clutching her ankles, and asked, "What do you want me to do?"

"I need to change," he said hurriedly. He was standing in the middle of the compartment with the suitcase open on the seat behind him. It was dark and although Timbers could see his figure stretching and bending, first with one foot on the seat then the other, she couldn't see clearly the clothes he was wearing.

"You haven't mentioned your wife?" she said, wanting to spoil the moment for him but she didn't hear his reaction. She remembered him saying, "We're going to miss it," and he turned to the window. Then a shock of light hit their little room. She saw him in his collarless shirt with red and white stripes. He had a cloth cap on his head and thick woollen braces were holding up his tweed trousers. He looked like a podgy apprentice boy at Blackpool. But the picture was gone in an instant.

The earth moved. A great sound, greater than a car crashing or a house falling down. It crushed the breath out of her. She closed her eyes tight and heard the torture of tearing metal that went on forever. Then came the screech of steel against steel, like a bomb screaming towards her. The ground moved again. Not a jolt, this time, but a breaking up that sent her to the floor. A dark shape like the shadow of a monstrous bird came close to the window. Scurries screamed, pointing at the horror. The two souls grabbed each other, differences forgiven, their frightened eyes searching for pity in the blackness. A great rumbling shook the ground and everything else. Their shoulders fell flat on the floor. In the middle of it all, Scurries managed to say, "You smell special." Timbers remembered it because it was an empty thing to say and because his voice seemed disengaged – loose in the air. Then a white flash – like the A-Bomb – scorched the sky with a fluorescence that burned their eyes long after it had gone. She reached for something to hold and opened her mouth to scream.

"This is your damned stupid fault!" yelled Scurries. "Your damned dithering and carping. Look what it's led to! Look what you've done! All of it wasted!"

He lunged at her, his thumbs going for her throat.

Timbers threw herself back onto the seat, brought her knees up to her chin and kicked out. Her two heels hit his chest and he went down squealing.

"For God's sake, a train's crashed out there!" she shouted. "You want to rape me while people are dying. Is that it? Get out!"

She kicked him on the floor. And again, so that when he crawled away, she was kicking him out of their little compartment.

"I knew you'd spoil it," he cried. He was in the corridor. Timbers saw him groping for the doorframe as he tried to get to his feet. With all her strength – and a great grunt – she slammed the sliding door onto his knuckles. He screamed with pain but she did it again.

"I'll murder you for this!" he shouted.

She wanted to chase him from the train but she was diverted by a woman's cry for help. She went to the carriage window and tugged at it until it gave just an inch or two. "I'm coming," she shouted. "I'll get people." She listened for a reply. It all sounded very quiet out there. Thank God, the late night train must have been almost empty, she thought. The woman called for help again; she hadn't heard Timbers' shouting.

Timbers left the compartment and felt her way along the corridor, her hands leaning on the coachwork. Her toes feeling for any holes in the floor. "Get out of my way, Fat-Mouse, if you're there." But she didn't see the Man from Scurries again that evening.

15

As she reached the last compartment in the coach, she noticed that something had been left on the seat. At first, it was just a grey shape in the darkness but when she stepped into the compartment, she realised that someone had abandoned a carrying cot. The moment was oddly peaceful in the middle of what was happening.

She hesitated. Timbers didn't like babies. She thought that they smelled badly and did horrible things to a woman's body. And getting close to them disturbed a conscience – and awoke the warning from the illegal abortionist that another visit to her back-parlour surgery would leave her 'in a state no good for anyone'.

Timbers wouldn't have touched the baby, but when she came close enough for him to make sense of her, she thought that his eyes seemed to talk to her. Definitely, he brightened when he saw her face. Definitely. She touched him and he made a noise but didn't cry. "Where's your mother?" she asked as plainly as if she expected the mite to reply.

She picked him up and held him close to her chest, laying a hand against his little back. His hair was too long around his ears, she noticed. He wanted to grow up to be a Beatle, she smiled. She cupped the back of his head in her hand and she felt his tummy muscles relax. He trusted her. She checked again that Scurries wasn't going to disturb them.

'You can't do this,' she told herself. His mother will want to take him away, won't she? God, there's been a train crash. She's not going to want him to be in danger, is she? Timbers, his mother will come back for him.

"It's too cold for you out there," she explained. "God, it's a train crash and no place for a baby like you." Carefully, she laid the little bundle in the cot and let a fingertip kiss his forehead. She promised to come back. She promised it, again and again, in her head.

In all tragedies, icy silence is the worst news. When Timberdick dropped awkwardly from the disused railway carriage to the cinder bed, she was brought up by the nearness of silhouettes shaped wrong in the night. She couldn't tell what went where because the wreck was almost upon her and the sky was too dark. But a train should be straight and level; this one jutted at angles. Black steel stuck out in every direction accentuating the 3D. Let no-one forget the power of this thing. But there was no shouting, no calling out, no crying for help. One sound brought a haunted chill to the silence. Somewhere loose iron was creaking like a desolate inn sign in a wicked place.

As she turned away from the carriage, Fred Leaper appeared from the greyness.

"I need someone to hold things for me," he said.

"There's a baby."

Fred Leaper's head was too full of the worst thing that had ever happened to him. He didn't hear her. "People are going to die, Miss, if we don't do something. Please-" As he came close enough to touch her, Timbers saw tears rolling down the old man's face. "Please. I've always said, Miss, if there's a crash, please God don't let Fred Leaper be on his own."

He took hold of her little hand.

"There's a baby in there."

This time, he heard the words but they didn't make sense to him. "That's all right, Miss. We'll find someone to look after the baby." Then he put things plainly, "Miss, there is no-one but you and me. I'm an old man who's no good anymore and you're a woman with no more strength than a tiddler-fish. But those people in that train – we're all they've got."

He told her to keep close as he guided her beneath the first of the carriages. The train was so wrecked that they could walk beneath it and hardly bend their backs. Tubes and shafts of woods were knitted above their heads. Cold wind rushed from the harbour into this phoney cavern. And there was no colour to anything, she noticed. Everything was grey. Something hot – water, oil? It didn't smell like petrol – dripped down Timbers' neck as she made her way beneath the carriage.

"There's a man from the first carriage – I've sat him on the grass bank, the other side. I'm afraid he looks pretty bad. And there's at least one more trapped in the middle carriage. No-one in the tail. Not as far as I can see. I've already checked the driver; he's all right. He's sitting with his daughter who came to meet him. Lucy, she's a good girl. She'll look after him. Now watch your step, Miss, because there's broken bits all over, and I'll show you what I need you to do." As she twisted and stretched her way through the wreckage, she could hear

17

Leaper going on, behind. "I can't do much, you see. Because of my ankles. They've been bad for days, you wouldn't believe them if I showed you. Horrid to mention it, I know. But you've got to know, haven't you?"

"I thought you said people were going to die?"

"Let me show you, Miss."

They emerged into the open air; it was thick with exhaust smoke and the smell of burnt oil. Timbers wanted to stop and make sense of things but Leaper, still holding her hand tight, made her trot along the side of the track. (All her life, men had been taking her to places.) "Don't look across the city, Miss. Don't look where things are all right. Our job's here, where we're the only ones who can help." At last, people were coming. Lights were on in the Station Road Hotel, sirens were approaching along different roads and a small crowd had gathered beneath the railway arches. They were shouting that they couldn't climb up the embankment. Something was blocking them. Neither Fred nor Timbers answered their calls.

"Never mind the people, Miss." He told her to get on her hands and knees. "I've got to get you underneath this last coach, you see." But the undercarriage had been forced so low and its chassis was so buckled that it was impossible to see between the train and the bed of chippings.

"No."

"You'll need to press yourself hard, Miss. Really press yourself into the stones. It's the only way that you'll get underneath."

"No."

"Just have a look for me."

She wanted to say no again. She crouched down so that her face was on the ground and looked under the train. "I can't go in there. We've got to wait for the firemen. God, what are you thinking? "

"That's right, Miss. You ask God, what's he thinking? You ask, what's he telling you to do?" Then his two hands gripped her bottom from behind and he pushed her into the darkness of more twisted metal. "I'm here, Miss. Here if you need me."

It was like being inside something evil. Like a burnt out furnace or a poisonous mine. She couldn't turn; she couldn't even look sideways. She couldn't crawl backwards. Like the little children made to go up

18

chimneys in olden days. "Keep going to the front," he shouted. Fred couldn't lay himself on the ground so his voice soon seemed far away from her. He shone his lamp as best he could and talked her through the dislodged wheels and spars of the undercarriage.

"You need to settle yourself firm against the bogie bars," he demanded. "Wedge yourself against the metal plate, like it's the back of a chair. I know what I want you to do, Miss, exactly. Please."

The knitting had been torn loose in her cardigan and her legs were bleeding. Her mini skirt had ridden up to her belt but still it was too tight; she wished she'd taken it off. She wished she'd taken her cardi off too, so that she could have used it as a cushion against things that hurt. She was busy with these grumbles when a metal nugget bit at her shoulder. She stopped, said nothing and gave herself some time to cry quietly. She hated her bony body; she was a skeleton with bits that stuck out at the corners. It never did her any good.

"I can't see the iron plate," she said petulantly.

"You don't understand."

Timbers had squeezed herself beneath the coupling and, by reaching up for the sprockets, had trapped herself. She couldn't move backwards or forwards.

"Then tell me," she called back. She managed to suck her grazed elbow but that's all she could do.

The railwayman said patiently, "The first two carriages are creeping. I can see them moving, an inch at a time. If you don't uncouple it, this last one's going to drag them down the embankment. They'll crash against the balustrade and break through, I'm sure, down to the road. See, you've got to break that coupling."

Timbers was looking hard at the mechanism. "Please, your torch is missing it. I need to work out which hose goes where."

He shifted the beam of yellow light. "Doesn't matter, Miss. You see the yellow hook-nut? It's like a handcuff only smaller and longer."

"Yes." It was nothing like handcuffs.

"Some wood's wedged it against the metal strut. Can you see?"

Timbers nodded to herself, then said yes to Fred.

"Bang it loose, Miss. We need you to bang it loose."

The train grunted, like a sick animal, and everything shifted another hand's width.

"Oh God, Missie," whined Fred Leaper. "Have a go at it for us."

"What will it do?"

"It'll put all the weight on the damaged coupling and break it free. Miss, just do it for us."

Sounds like rubbish, said a voice in her head. She argued, "But then the carriage will roll down the embankment."

"It won't. It'll settle. I know it will." But there was no certainty in his voice, only desperation.

"Will it crush me?"

There was an awkward pause. Without a word, they both acknowledged that, probably, the train would move on to her little body.

Her eyes were sticky with tears. This wasn't her job, she wanted to say.

"Love, a lot of people will die if these carriages crash through the balustrade and into the houses."

"Can't you think of a better way?" she asked.

Fred said sorry. His ideas were all they had. Probably, he was doing things wrong, but they couldn't wait for people with better ideas. "I'm going to see if I can find a jack, Miss. I won't be long." He added, "You keep talking to me. Even though I'm not here, you keep going on."

How had she got into this? Why were an old man and a skinny whore trying to save people in a train crash? "How long have I been in here?" she called but the old man wasn't there to answer. She was crying properly now, not sobbing but steadily. "I wanted to tell you about the baby," she said quietly. "You know, if this bloody train falls on me and God says, 'What's the last thing you want to do, Timbers, for ten seconds before you die.' I'd say, hold that baby, Sir. I just want to hold that little baby for a moment."

Then she thought, talking to yourself? Does that mean you really are going to die? Is that what people do?

She heard the stones move at the side of the train as Leaper knelt down. "The firemen are trying to get to us," he called. "They've got to come up from the sportsground. You see, even they say the bridge is unsafe, so they're going the long way round. But the ground's too soft to get the equipment up. It'll take some time, their officer said."

"Did you tell them where I am?"

"No, Miss," Leaper confessed. "No, I didn't tell them that."

"Did you tell anyone about the baby?"

"Oh yes. Didn't you hear me shout it?"

No, Leaper. No, because you're lying.

"Leaper, go and get that baby. Now." She wanted to explain her feelings, but she knew that he wouldn't listen. She muttered to herself, "God, you don't understand."

Her hips ached from being so long in a wrong position. She tried to stretch, and had to push against small rocks and turf that had slipped from the bank at the side of the track. She managed to straighten one leg, but then something fell on her foot as it protruded from the wreckage. She kicked; the obstacle moved but fell back on her. She kicked again and, this time, bent her neck so that she could see the other end of her body.

She screamed. Her foot was pressed into a dead man's face.

"It's all right, pet."

"It's not!"

"It's the man on the bank. He died. I didn't think he was hurt so badly."

"Move him!"

"I'm trying to, love."

"Move him!"

"Yes."

Then vomit filled her mouth and bubbled from her lips like porridge boiling over. She thought she was going to choke. Then, a wrenching convulsion propelled the sick out of her.

She thought he had gone away again, old man Leaper with the bad ankles. Then she heard his voice, much weaker than it had been. He wasn't so sure of things. "I've found some wood, Love."

"What good is that?"

"I thought, if you could find somewhere to wedge it. Perhaps." But he didn't believe it.

He said, "Do you want me to get you out?"

Timbers wanted, more than anything in her life, to stop weeping. She felt that all the unfairness in her life had been planned to bring her to this moment. Everything bad that she had done would be put right if she could do things properly for the next two minutes. Just be

21

grown-up, she said to herself. Just show, in the end, that you were what you were supposed to be. She knew, perhaps like soldiers know seconds before they run into fire, that she was probably going to die. God, she wanted to do it right.

"Or wait for help? Perhaps we could wait," said Leaper, quietly throwing her a lifeline. But everything in his voice said that getting out and waiting were the wrong things to do.

"The man's all right now. You can look. You can't see him. I've laid him by the side of the track."

"You mean he's alive?"

"No, Miss. He's still dead."

The train shifted again. Timbers screamed, very shortly, and began to pant. "I can do it," she called out. Already she had a stone in her hand and was pushing it up to her face so that she could strike the 'hook-nut'. Can't be called that, she thought as she hit it the first time. Can't be called that, and on the second strike, it fractured.

Oh God! It can't be called that because it's not the hook-nut! I've broken the wrong thing!

She heard air exploding, metal snapping and a great crunch as the carriages moved with their own weight. She screamed. As loud as she could scream. The last carriage rolled towards her – just as it should have done – and she buried her face in her hands as she stayed flat on the track and waited for God to decide if she had been a good girl or not.

Three

The Way of an Old Town Copper

At three in the morning, I was shaking hands with the door handles of London Road. 239 down to 78. The new Sergeant wanted lock-up shops to be checked once before refs and again afterwards. This instruction suited me, because pretended suspicion of intruders on premises provided the best excuse to slip around the backs for a smoke. Recently, the roof of the Westminster Bank had become one of my favourite stops. I could see the length of London Road from there and still keep an eye on the back twitchels. The brick boiler shaft, with overhanging eaves and slatted wood shutters, offered warmth on a cold night.

I hadn't realised how easy it was to reach the roof until young Fraser Stephens, with less than nine months in, showed me. Then he demonstrated the probationers' latest sport. Hiding behind the phoney balustrade, he shone his torch on the street below. With a little practice, he explained, a chap could guide the beam to meet the tarmac just where the light from a passing cyclist's lamp hits the ground. Then he could prompt the reflections to diverge. The perpetrator scored one point if the surprised cyclist wobbled, three if he called out and five if he fell off. And a massive ten points if the victim went to the police station and complained about delinquent policemen. I told young Stephens off. The prank was dangerous and disreputable and he had better tell his probationer friends to keep off the Westminster's roof. Or they'd answer to me.

Having checked numbers 239 down to 120, I climbed to the top of the bank, confident that I would have the place to myself. I took off my black cloak, made a cushion of it and propped myself against the chimneystack. I heard the fire engine's bell as it tracked the course of the old creek on the edge of the city. I guessed that the city's appliances were busy with other incidents and the chiefs had called in crews from the county divisions. I looked about but could see no smoke. Probably, something was wrong in the harbour and the dock-yard police had sought help from the civvies.

I filled a pipe bowl with Rennie Tegg's special mixture of tobacco and, gently, drawing just enough, got it going. Then, I reached behind the chimneystack for two bottles of Mackeson and an opener.

* * *

I had joined the Police Force in 1937, having driven Fodens and Albions between Eastleigh and Leighton for four years. From the start, I was no good as a copper. I wasn't quick enough on my feet and earned a reputation for arriving too late at scenes of crimes. Colleagues thought that being paired with PC Machray was bad news and, for a time, they called me Inky. Short for Stinky. When I was eighteen months into the job, one of Maxwell Knight's men came down to the south coast and asked for an aide to carry satchels and open doors. My Sergeant said that the local station wouldn't miss me. So, I became a plain-clothes policeman with less than two years in. Almost a detective you could have said. I thought it was an industrial burglary case; I didn't realise that Knight was a spycatcher and his men were investigating sabotage. They were a strange lot and they played hard. They were always asking me for local gossip and I was always sorry that I didn't know any. Then I got drunk one night in the Blacksmith's Arms and talked for hours about the antics I had seen in road haulage. I made a bit of a twerp of myself, I'm afraid, because no-one wanted to listen to me. Everyone wanted to wait on a dark haired woman who had come down from London for the evening. My colleagues showed her great deference, but no-one told me that she was the main witness in one of MI5's most important espionage trials. Everyone must have been embarrassed by my twitterings but I was too tipsy to notice. I quickly forgot the episode, but in 1940 I was drafted into one of Knight's satellites in the War Office. I was supposed to advise the military on how the fifth column could hide things on lorries and ferry them about the country. It was good fun, watching skulduggery from the sidelines, although I always thought that I was advising people other than the military about things other than freight haulage. The trouble was that I didn't want to be a spycatcher. In fact, I've never wanted to be much at all.

The months before D Day were a golden time, I remember. I had been told to roam around East Anglia, drink in as many pubs as I could cope with, and let the beer loosen my tongue. They wanted me to play the fool as part of a greater game. (I can see that now.) I was in my mid-thirties, there was a war on and I spent many afternoons drunk in the corners of cornfields.

The job died with the end of the war but the Police Force wouldn't take me back. I worked as a hotel porter for two years, then asked again. This time, I persuaded my boss in MI5 to insist that the Chief Constable had to accept me because I had been drafted to the War Office for hostilities only.

Those were good days for policemen. A beat Bobby's job was to sort things out on the street. No-one thanked you for bringing work back to the station or calling your superiors too close to the action. So, each policeman became a lone sheriff with his own way of working. Unfortunately, this meant that the Sergeants had little to do and were always looking for mischief. They chased the young 'uns hard, but learned to leave me alone.

I was past it. Throughout the 1950's, I kept out of harm's way, plodding from one tea stop to the next, laughing and joking in people's back rooms. Then in 1963, a stupid Superintendent decided that Tommy 'Stand-by' Moreton and I should do permanent nights. The local Watch Committee had read the Denning report and resolved to clean up the city's morals. Our job – Tommy and I – was to sort out the tarts on Goodladies Road. We didn't, of course.

Dog litter on the pavements offended Tommy. This was a time when no-one else took any notice of it but Tommy had time to think about it on nights. He started a one-man campaign, encouraging kids to tell Mums and Dads 'not to do it' and convincing the community to designate the waste ground behind Shelton's motor garage as a dog walking pitch. People chuckled at his enthusiasm for such inconsequential business and crude cartoons began to appear on the Police Station's notice boards but, really, 'Stand-by' was years ahead of his time.

While Tommy worried about the state of the pavements, I would spend the small hours in Jack's All Night Café. My friend with the Ministry had learned that Jack was showing political films on his home cinema outfit and he wanted me to identify the people who came to watch. When I said that no dissident group would accept a policeman, especially in uniform, he scoffed. "You're fat, Ned. They'll think you're as thick as fog and twice as dense. Besides, you joined the Labour Party in '61." (This was his way of warning me that my old firm was keeping an eye on me as well as Jack's dissidents.) [1]

Then, in time for Christmas 1963, the stupid Superintendent died. My superiors knew that I had hated the man; I had even joked that I wanted to have a hand in his dispatch. Unfortunately, I was alone at his hospital bedside when he passed away, so the A.C.C. was pleased to suspend me while the death was investigated. He brought in a Deputy Chief Constable from another county – who promptly declared that any notion of foul play was preposterous. For a second time in my career, the Police Force had to take me back reluctantly. "Creep through the back door," said the new officer-in-charge. "And don't tell anyone you're back." I remember his colourful instruction: Keep to the alleyways and don't come out 'til night. "And PC Machray, I don't want to hear anything about you."

On the Westminster's roof, I took my time. I allowed the sounds of the city at night to comfort me. Boats still moved in the harbour, railway engines were shunting tonight in the freight yards and a fire engine was racing down the distant arterial road, past the yachts in shallow water, past the engineering factories that worked all night and the roundabout that was big enough for cricket.

The fire engines, I counted three of them, said that something was wrong in the city but I was sure that the emergency was none of my business. Very little was to do with me; I had four bottles of stout and three pipefuls of Rennie's Russian and Liquorice Mixture in my head.

---

[1] It hasn't occurred to me before. Jack's film club could have been the real reason for my night duties. Perhaps it had nothing to do with the girls. When I reported that Jack's audience was interested in stag films, not propaganda, my sponsor arranged for me to introduce some left wing material and observe reactions. We will never know the truth; I am in my eighties and everyone else is dead.

I was woolgathering. Characters from ten years ago came to meet me. Conversations in pubs that had been pulled down long ago were as fresh as teatime's tele. I thought about the hidden places – the back-yards, the alleys and dark street corners – where I had learned what it meant to live in a dirty city.

With the beer in my head, I dozed. I remembered the night, four years before, when Betty 'Slowly' Barnes came to my room and wept because she thought policemen were after her. She was already earn-ing her living on the pavements of Goodladies Road but the rossers meant not to arrest her but to taunt her about ghosts and bogeys. I told her they were crackers and, to prove that nothing bad was out there, we spent the night in St Mary's bell tower and made up stories from the sounds we heard. Until morning.

On another night, three years before Betty's, I had wandered through the graveyard, my copper's torch loose at my side, and saw a spindly girl sleeping on the doorstep of St Mary's Vestry. She was a runaway, she said. For eleven years, she had been waiting for some-one to come looking for her. Did I know, she asked, that a city full of people could be the loneliest place in the world? I folded my police coat over her cold, bony shoulders and sat with her for an hour, smoking and looking about and talking only a little. I left her there because she had nowhere else to go. (I first met Timbers in 1957 and I asked her to marry me in 1963. Silly soft sod, said the canteen ladies. Timbers said no. She had grumbled about me ever since and told me off when she was cross, but I was the one she trusted.)

These memories got muddled with others.

The clattering bell of the area patrol car shook me awake. Surely, I couldn't have been properly asleep! Not me, who was expert at cat-napping. I rubbed my wristwatch as if the rubbing would produce some magic to turn back the clock. I knew I was late. But when I crawled to the edge of the balustrade and put the watch in the light of the lamps below, I saw that I was in real trouble. I had missed two patrol points!

I got to the police phone, on the corner of Hawkins. I unlocked the cast iron hutch and dialled the station.

Inspector Hillier answered. She said, "I've booked you sick, Ned."

"Grief. Jennie what are you doing there?"

"There's been a train crash."

"What are you saying Jen? Do what?"

"They've called me in. There's been a train crash, Ned. They sent me down to the Royal to count the bodies but there was only one – and Timbers who was locked in the toilets – so they said I had to take over the front office at Central."

The story came in a rush. I pressed the telephone closer to my ear, trying to get more sense out of it. I kept saying, what? Do what? Then I jumped with surprise as the first of the bread vans raced past and the bright yellow Bedford of the Express and Star. The van doors were open and the driver was sticking to low noisy gears.

She shouted down the phone. "A train crash, I said."

I asked if people had been hurt.

"Not many. Not half a dozen, I think. But they've closed the roads to the ferry and it would have been much worse if Fred hadn't acted so quickly. The man's a hero."

I told her that I was late calling in and she asked what excuse I was going to use.

I offered the one about saving a cat from strangulation. "I swear the damned thing wanted to kill herself."

She laughed but said that no-one would notice my missing patrol points. "You need to keep out of the way for a few days, Ned. The Superintendent came here an hour ago, stamping and shouting and wanting to know if you were drinking on top of the Westminster Bank. That's when I said it couldn't have been you, because you reported in sick before refs."

"Did he believe you?"

"He didn't have time to think about it, dear. He's with everyone else, down at the Station Road bridge. If Fred Leaper hadn't acted so bravely, three carriages would have dropped to the crossroads. Virtually held them back with his own strength. Imagine it, Ned."

I couldn't. I couldn't imagine anyone holding back a railway carriage with his own strength. It sounded nonsense from the start.

The streets were empty again. Somewhere, a sash window clattered shut, a cat upturned a bin lid and a boiler fired. These were the unconnected sounds of a city not yet ready to wake.

Then Jennie told me about Timberdick. "The hospital wouldn't take her, so I called the Hoboken woman but she wouldn't open up either. She wanted to know what the tripe was doing on railway lines at one in the morning."

"Tripe, Jen? She called her tripe?"

"Trollop. That was it. What was the trollop doing there in the first place, she said. I got one of the taxi's to pick her up in the end. You'd better get round to her place, Ned. But Lord knows the state she's in."

I checked my watch. It would take me twenty minutes to reach Timber's flat off the Nore Road. "I won't get back in time to clock off," I said. "You'll have to cover my half four and five o'clock points."

"Don't worry about that. The skipper's out. I said, everyone's down at the station." Fred was a hero, she said, and made me listen to the story again.

I didn't hurry. A good policeman never gets out of breath, people had told me, so I had learned the studied amble, almost a dawdler's march, that enabled the Constable to negotiate every obstacle without altering his pace and hardly altering his course. I followed the trolley bus lines down London Road to the junction with St Mary's, then cut through the cemetery to the nub of the Nore Road.

Timbers lived in a terraced house fifty yards from the main street. Mrs Miller owned the house and lived on the middle floor. D'Olivera had the rooms in the attic and the veranda, which gave Timbers the ground floor and the front and back doors. The yard was everyone's but Timbers had the back step – often she would sit there on bright days with her bare feet on the cracked concrete. Sometimes she'd set the outside tap trickling over her toes. Mrs Miller had asked her not to bring her men back to the house.

I hesitated on her doorstep. I didn't want the doorbell to wake her and, if she was already awake, she probably wouldn't answer the door. So I let myself in with the key she had given me. I heard her washing in the tiny kitchen that was an alcove from the living room. A bare bulb above the sink offered some dim lighting to the room. Quietly, I moved an armchair into the middle of the room and sat down.

A trail of discarded clothes had fallen where she had stripped off on her way to the kitchen. Then she had laid a dirty hand towel on the floorboards in front of the sink, so that she could wash herself with soap and a flannel and the suds would fall on the towel. She was over-doing it, rubbing more and more soap in to the cloth and lathering her backside and between her legs, her soles and toes and under her arms (but never the back of her neck), until she was covered in soapy foam. This wasn't the first time I had seen her without clothes. I had often put her to bed when she wasn't sensible enough to manage herself. But I hadn't looked at her for six months and the sight saddened me. Her little body used to have the stridency and impertinence of her personality but it had a worn and weary look now. She used to make jokes about her square bottom and coathanger shoulders; now they looked like old women's muscles. (God, she's only thirty-four. She should look nothing like this, I thought.)

She became aware of my presence only gradually. She continued to wash every bit of her (but not her neck) vigorously but not so rudely or ruggedly. She allowed herself a little flirtiness, as if she wanted me to recognise the temptress that was still buried inside her.

She dried herself with the towel from the floor, then threw it aside, then changed her mind and, when she walked into the sitting-room, she was clutching the hand-towel to her front; it was big enough to cover everything it needed to – just about.

"I used to have a nice old gentleman who watched me wash and powder myself while he remembered things from the Bible. 'And it came to pass in an evening tide,' he used to chant. He used to sit there with his hands on top of his belly, and give off this bit he'd learned about a king who went on to his roof and saw a woman washing."

"And the woman was very beautiful to look upon," I contributed.

"Hey, you know it? What was her name?"

"Lord knows."

"Bathsheba," she said, happy that I had failed the test. Then, in quiet explanation, "I know because I had to play the part for him. I was supposed to be someone's wife and he spied on me. I always thought it had a fruity touch for a Bible story. He killed the other man, of course."

"The man did?"

She smiled at my alarm. "Not my gentleman, you dumb plod, the man in the Bible. He fixed for the girl's husband to be killed in battle.

Then God let their baby die because he'd been born in sin. He used to tell me the story, my gentleman did, while I was washing with nothing on. It always got me wondering what God felt about me. It'd explain a lot."

"Your man was very lucky."

"You were looking at me funny," she said. "You didn't think that I was 'beautiful to look upon'. I could see you thinking things, weren't you Ned? You've noticed that things are wrong with me. That I'm old. It used to be just the paintwork that was wrong but now it's rot. I'm rotting, Ned."

"Hey, I was thinking nothing of the sort. Your bloke last night, he wanted you to spend all night in a train. He didn't think you were rotten, did he? And nice old Mo was telling me how you looked at the top of Old Moore's Lane. You're still a 'wow', Timbers."

"I've done something bad."

"Jennie said you locked yourself in the toilets."

"Bugger Jennie."

"Did you?"

"I was at the hospital. I kept telling the nurses about my baby but they wouldn't believe me. Every time I said it, they came back and said they'd checked; he wasn't there. So, I locked myself in."

"Don't worry about it now," I said.

"I kept it up for a hour, you know. Just like when I was a kid." She settled herself on the carpet and folded her arms on my lap. "I've done something bad," she repeated. "It's never going to go away. It's going to get bigger and bigger and will probably spoil my whole life."

"Your whole life?" I tickled the tufts of short hair on the back of her neck. "Goodness."

"Don't molly-coddle me, Ned. You know I won't take it. Listen to me, there was a baby boy on the train and I left him there."

"His mother would have found him, surely."

"Didn't see her," she mumbled after a pause. She busied her fingers with something on the carpet. Picking, rubbing, rolling it between her fingers. She tried hard to explain her feelings. "I don't like babies, you know that. It's not about wanting to cuddle him in my arms or feed him, or see his smile. It's about Timberdick Woodcock doing what's right, even when nobody's bloody interested. The way it is – I've walked away. Now, what do I do? Do I go back and look for him? My mother didn't come looking for me, did she? I've been waiting on the bloody street corners, with my skirt up round my arse, for eighteen years and she never came. That's what this is about. That's why I'm sitting on this bloody floor, crying, getting my face all red again. Do I turn up for this baby, or do I let you molly-coddle me?"

It was nonsense, of course. But you don't tell Timbers off for being silly. You don't offer her coffee and a handkerchief or reassure her with reason. You come to her, and sit quietly and still, and touch her gently when she wants you to. I sensed that she was thinking through what had happened. I knew that Timbers was a careful thinker, for all her bluster and stubbornness. She liked to tell herself stories in her head until she understood what was important, what was trivial and what could be forgotten (or may not have happened).

When she was ready, I laid my hand on her shoulder. "What can you do about it, Timbers? Search the city?"

She thought about that, then nodded, "O.K. You're a policeman. You do it. Find him for me and tell me he's all right."

I went to the kitchenette, looked for a tin of Cross and Blackwell soup and warmed the contents before pouring it into cereal bowls. Timbers turned up her nose; she always did. I rained pepper over mine and stood on the hearthrug as I sucked it noisily from the spoon.

"Did you see the other passenger?" I asked.

She nodded. "The curly headed witch from the dress shop on the Nore Road."

"Bellamy?"

She nodded. "Brenda"

"Barbara."

"Betty."

"Barbara," I insisted. "Did she tell you what had happened?"

She shook her head. "I just saw her being led up the grass bank as I crawled from under the train."

I said, "There are too many questions about Fred Leaper's part in all this. For a start, he didn't carry the weight of a railway carriage. Neither did you. If he knew people were hurt in the train – a man was dying, for God's sake – surely he would have taken you to them. To see if you could help. Instead, he hid you under the carriage."

"He didn't hide me," Timbers protested. "He needed me to stop the train falling over."

"No Timbers. Come on, even you didn't believe that at the time. That's what you've said. And he's told everyone that he'd saved the train, not you."

"He wants to be famous," she said unconvincingly.

I drew breath, "And I want to know why Scurries took so long getting to Moore's Lane? Where was he while you were standing by the café drainpipe, getting cold, getting cross."

"You spoke to Mo in the café?"

I nodded. "She doesn't trust him at all."

* * *

I left Timbers sleeping at ten o'clock. I dawdled through the grey Edwardian streets. The dirty clouds in the sky gave a pearly reflection in the puddles and the people walked with their heads down, shoulders hunched and their arms close to their bodies. The men who wore hats, although nowhere else was it fashionable, pulled the edges down to their ears.

Two lads who worked on the ferries had opened a record shop on the corner of Cardrew Street and Rossington. It was an end of terrace house that they had painted yellow and bright orange. They had sell-otaped l.p. covers to the insides of the windows and they kept the front door open. An old borstal boy was sitting on the step picking at a battered Telecaster, not plugged in.

"Hey, there, Mr Ned!" (I had left my tit-for at Timbers' place and wore a civvie jacket over my thick blue shirt but people could see that I was a copper in uniform.) He called as he went on strumming, "Your bird got any more Bo Diddley?" He meant Jennie, not Timbers. Jennie knew nothing about jazz and blues but she had found a second-hand Pye International e.p. and I had passed it on to Sean.

"None that you haven't already got," I replied simply.

"Yeah, Mr Ned, she's a real cat, your bird."

I made him nudge up so that I could sit beside him on the step. It was too low for me and my rear was too broad to perch comfortably on the concrete. He stopped playing the guitar, rolled two cigarettes and handed one to me.

"Bo Diddley's not real jazz, Sean," I said. "He's hardly blues."

"Yeah? So what's real jazz, Mr Ned?"

He was expecting this old codger to come up with something out-of-date. I didn't disappoint. "Jazz is five boys in a hotel room in the 1920's. They work in the orchestras each night but come together after the shows and play the music they've learned from black records. Room 1411 is one, by Benny Goodman's Boys with Jimmy and Glen."

"Yeah? His boys, eh?"

"People who'd come and go. People like the Dorseys and Red Nichols. They'd be leading their own bands in five years, but these were the days when they were working hard at it, not just dreaming, but learning good jazz."

"Yeah. Like The Beatles in Hamburg."

No, I said. Nothing like The Beatles in Hamburg.

I sucked on the cigarette. "So what's going on upstairs, Sean?"

"Say! Who says there's anything?"

"You're standing sentry, Sean, and you keep shouting 'Mr Ned' so everyone knows I'm here. Perhaps I should go inside and look?"

"Hey, no. There ain't a need. It's just two of the boys entertainin' Baz Shipley, and I'm here in case old Ma Shipley comes looking for her. Ma doesn't like Baz playing in concerts."

"How does Baz feel about it?" I asked.

"Hey, Mr Ned, it's a business matter. Buyin' and sellin', i'n't it?"

An upstairs window tattled open and Baz's giggling cleared any suspicion that Sean was trying to fool me. Baz Shipley, the youngest and perhaps the best looking of Timbers' crowd, was working in the mornings, unusually – it was something that the girls didn't do around the Hoboken. Sean helped me to my feet and I crossed the road so that Baz could see me from the window. (She didn't shout for help. Well, she wouldn't, would she?)

I dropped into the back of the Seaman's Sandwich Bar for a free breakfast and reached Shooter's Grove before two. The Divisional Training School had been converted from a posh house on the corner. Jennie Hillier was in charge of it. She was supposed to have two Sergeants and a classroom of probationary Constables, but the

Sergeants were usually deployed elsewhere and probationers were sent out of the division for training. However, the A.C.C. (Admin) insisted that the Training School must remain open and an Inspector retained in post. It was a non-job.

Between eight o'clock and half past five Inspector Jennie busied herself with routines so faithfully that they took on the sanctity of rituals. Habits not to be broken. She entered by the front door, having secured the garden gate with a loop of string, and brought in the milk. Then she checked each room for intrusion or accidents. High ceilings, closed fireplaces, cold and – no matter how she tried to decorate the place – bare and empty looking rooms. Then she returned to the front door, collected the post from the mat and left it in a pile on her desk – on the second floor, overlooking the back garden, the creek and the playing fields beyond. Only then, did she attend to the kettle and the tea tray.

Exile did have its pleasures. She liked to take lunch and afternoon tea in the back garden. And some days, she arrived early so that she could soak in the bath on the first floor. The water at Shooter's Grove was excitingly hot and no-one counted the cost. Other days, she stayed late so that she could change before going out. Usually alone. Often to the theatre.

Sometimes she thought Ned Machray was her best friend.

She knew that she had to endure this exile because important people unfairly blamed her for the death of the mad Superintendent. She insisted that the exile didn't mean that she was washed-up. She found ways of pretending she was more busy than she was. She was always careful to allow a delay before answering the telephone and her diary was always too full, she said, to agree to a meeting on the date of first choice. But her favourite trick was to move the dates of the required $3^1/_2$ training days each month because of unforeseen, and unexplained, circumstances.

The doors were locked when I got to Shooter's Grove but I knew that she wouldn't be out.

"Lord above. Have you been to bed? Neddie, look at the state of you." Women had been saying that to me since I was old enough to understand. Mothers and Nannas, teachers and a sequence of girlfriends had been unable to influence my appearance; I always looked

35

to be on the point of falling apart. "Do you want a nap in the bunk room?" Jennifer asked.

The bunkroom was a cold cabin of six stacked beds at the top of the house. They were designated accommodation for reserve sections in case of nuclear attack. Their authority came from the same A.C.C. (Admin.) who had determined that Jen should sit in her office, doing next to nothing between eight-thirty and five each day. Certainly, no Civil Defence protocol required the availability of six beds. The A.C.C. wanted to be sure that the facility wasn't abused, so Jen kept a hardbacked register in her office. The book was empty, of course, and the beds were often used by the locked-out husbands, legless Sergeants and cadets-in-trouble that populated our division.

"I'm on the sick," I reminded her. I would have plenty of time to sleep that evening. "But I'd go for a bath, Jennie."

A sudden frostiness snagged her face. The bath was her's and fat Ned Machray – especially when he had been up all night and probably drinking – was not the sort of person that she wanted soaking in it. Frankly, she couldn't be sure where I'd been or what I might have picked up.

"Of course, it's not important," I said.

Jennie recovered her manners. "No, please, Ned. It will refresh you. Go and run it while I sort out some towels from the airing cupboard."

Inspector Jen's bath was an old enamelled one on legs. It had taps the size of submarine cocks and a brass plug on a brass chain. Leaving the bathroom door open, so that the Mistress of Shooter's Grove would have no doubt that she could enter without embarrassment; I turned the hot tap full on. Immediately, the room began to fill with steam from the scalding water.

"There's some Dettol under the sink," she pointed out. "Splash some in the water, if you like." Disinfectant helped her cope with my trespass. Then her phone rang, she retreated to the office and, very thankful, I attended to the business of the bath.

Now, call me odd (I'm sure you will) but I do like to sit on the edge of a bath with my feet in the hot water, while drawing on a pipe of dampened tobacco. So, I started to set things up. I took my shoes and socks off. I locked the door and took off my trousers. I took the pipe from my jacket pocket and I held the tobacco over the steam while I filled the bowl. I stuck it in my mouth and I tested the bathwater. Fine. I put one foot in, placed my white panted bottom on the rim (it was too big for it, frankly) and carefully brought the other leg over the top. Good. But as soon as I was ready to light up, Jennie shouted from the office. "God Ned! It's murder!"

Then she was thumping on the bathroom door and calling me out. "Ned, the man in the train was murdered. The train crash didn't kill him. He was knifed in the neck. Murder on the line from London, Ned."

So, I climbed out the bath, put my wet feet and ankles through my trouser legs and unlocked the door.

"Central C.I.D.'s just phoned me," she said. "They want me to question Timberdick."

Four

Dancing to the Maple Leaf Rag

Only the Hoboken did ragtime in 1964. The pubs were full of Mersey music and rhythm and blues. True, Timmy Tornado still dressed in his pink drapes and brothel creepers and sang rock 'n' roll at the Blueberry on Thursdays. And people still spoke about the trad craze two years before and posters for folk music regularly appeared on the boarded windows and bus shelters. But Timmy Tornado was a curiosity, no-one bought jazz 45's and the folk clubs were a long way from our part of town. So, it was The Beatles and The Rolling Stones and only the Hoboken did ragtime.

With a piano, a drum and the navy's best fiddle player, Gimlet and Peach played Scott Joplin on the Goodladies Road after lights out. Because the doors were locked and it was probably not allowed, and because the music had forbidden roots and no-one else played it, the Hoboken had the magical feel of a speakeasy on those Tuesday nights. Chloed – say 'Clo' and whisper the 'd', she told everyone – had paid eighty pounds for the picture over the bar. Sonny Britches had painted it on cracked plaster and made it look old. He called it The Medicine Show and said it showed girls with men in top hats in a Western saloon. Chloed said it looked more like Paris but she loved it just the same. Men and old women would sit on bar stools and blow kisses at the floosies on the wall. But the best of the atmosphere came from the music. 'Lemon' Gimlet understood that ragtime should be played slowly, just as Joplin had wanted it, so that the ragged time stood out and made the dancer want to lop this way and then that. Rolling drunk is the best way to move with ragtime and the Hoboken at four in the morning had a lot of that.

Chloed was clever. She knew how to sell nightlife. Certainly, the

38

Hoboken on Tuesdays felt like a speakeasy but Chloed had a pukka licence for the late night drinking and music. Let no-one mention it, mind. She kept her permission well hidden and liked to get everyone nervy about a raid. The uncertainty meant atmosphere. But the law didn't worry her. "Nothing's in here as shouldn't be," she told the lady Police Inspector as she pulled her pint with too much froth on it. A Cornish childhood had laid a warmth in her vowels but she didn't linger on them.

Chloed was a quick woman. She went from one end of the bar to the other, from one room to the next, from this corner to that one, like a pointer bitch unable to decide its favourite spot in a new house. The gambling went on in private parties upstairs and there were plenty of stories about the buying and selling of underworld debts. One thing Chloed insisted upon; the girls could not put themselves on offer. What went on the private rooms was private business, but she wouldn't have them standing their wares in bars and corridors.

Inspector Jennie wasn't quick to understand this caution. She asked, "Where's Timberdick?"

"I don't know. But if you see her, tell her to stop sending under age girls into my pub. A young lady was asking for her, not half an hour ago, and she couldn't have been two months out of school. Far too innocent to be in an alehouse like this. She said please and thank you. I sent her away, of course. I told her to go and look somewhere else."

"So where's Timbers?"

"I like to keep an eye on her and she was in here, but I'm not sure. Outside, perhaps, but you stay here in the warm. I'll get someone from the kitchen to go and look for her." Chloed turned to a slovenly dressed woman who was sitting on a barstool. "Are you busy, Bet?"

Betty 'Slowly' Barnes was drunk. She managed to stay on the stool by pressing her elbows hard on the counter. She tried to focus her eyes on the gin that she held between her hands. She said, "I'm waiting."

"I won't have you picking up blokes in here," said Chloed.

"He's not a bloke. He's a friend." Gingerly, Betty dipped her head as she conceded, "He's not a gentleman, no, but a friend."

"Well, I want you to find Timberdick for the Inspector here."

"I don't have to." She turned to the policewoman. "Do you know what I do, these days? I beat the bald bottoms of bored men." Then, after just a moment's consideration, "Do you think I'm clever? All those b's in a row and I didn't fall over them. Baldly beating bored bottoms."

"Can you go and find Timbers?"

"I don't have to."

Chloed had already signalled the cellarman, who arrived to take gentle hold of Betty's sleeve.

"I don't have to, because I know where she is."

* * *

Timberdick Woodcock and a merchant navy man had completed their business in an upstairs room. She sat naked on the bed, her feet barely touching the cold carpet, and lit a cigarette. He had left the room for a pee, dressed in his trousers and leather belt and Chelsea boots but leaving his shirt and socks on the bed. Now, she could hear him barracking a card game in the room next door. She put on his shirt, made sure that the money was safely locked in the dressing table and wandered on to the landing.

Baz Shipley was sitting on the windowsill overlooking the dray yard. She wore crisp white lingerie and the best stilettos that Timbers had ever seen.

"He's an arsehole, yours is," the younger girl muttered as Timbers came next to her. "Layna had a bugger of a do with him, three nights ago."

Poor Layna, both girls thought.

"You look good standing out here," Timbers said. "You've got the legs for it. Stockings, corsets, high heels. You've legs like an antelope. I've always said it."

"Rennie Tegg wants me to throw for the A's this Wednesday night, Timbers. What d'you think of that, eh? I shouldn't be up here, you know. I should be downstairs practising. Still, Wednesdays – I've told Arnie that I can't go through it with his new strippers at the night-club; I've got to get down here early and get my eye in."

Timbers had learned to be patient with the younger girl's

enthusiasms. In another week, she would have lost interest in darts. "What did Arnie say to that?" she asked.

"He said, don't tell Marje. She'll go burlesque."

"Burlesque? Is that what he said?"

"That's what he said. Still, playing darts can be for, like, forever, can't it? You see old girls of seventy or eighty throwing every week, don't you?"

Well, thought Timbers. No you don't. And the men only want you to play because you've got good legs.

"Look, I'm good at darts and tarting. Darts is Wednesday nights and Sundays, which leaves six nights and six days for the other. That's how I see it. And I won't be doing tarting forever. My mum stopped when she was thirty. O.K., she started taking in cripples at fifty, but she stopped – I mean, she showed that a girl can stop doing it. She's always saying, 'I'm sure you'll grow out of it, Beryl.' This is what I'm going to do. Find someone who likes me, then I'll say to him, right, you don't have to marry me but I'm stopping for you."

Baz took hold of Timbers' cigarette and drew on it before passing it back. "The girl detective's downstairs. She's been asking about you."

"She'll want to bloody lock me up, you know that. She never wants to do anything else." The two girls turned their backs to the landing of bedrooms. "What do you think, Baz?" Timbers asked as they looked out of the window. "One hand on the drainpipe, the other on the windowsill until I lose my grip and drop on the dustbins?"

The younger girl laughed. "I'd get some clothes on first."

"Yes, if I'm going to be picked up by the fuzz." After a moment's quiet, she said, "Bloody Jennifer Hillier."

"And I'd leave by the kitchen, not the window. It'd sound better in court."

"Bloody Jennifer Hillier," Timbers said again.

She returned to the bedroom and gathered her skirt and sleeveless cardi from the bottom of the bed. She was about to drop the seaman's shirt to the carpet when the door swung open.

"Bugger," she said, turning to face her visitor and sure that she was nicked.

D.I. Hillier hesitated on the threshold. She shifted her weight from one foot to the other and brushed some fallen hair from her face. "Would you like me to give you a few minutes?"

"I'd like you to piss off," said Timbers.

"Look, I can't help it, I'm supposed to talk with you." She bothered with her hair again. "Look, you're not in trouble."

"Only because it doesn't suit you at the moment. What do you want?"

Miss Hillier kept trying. "Can we sit on the bed?"

"The bed? Me and you?"

"While we talk, Timbers. Look, we can sit wherever you want. I'll stand, if you like."

Like a child showing off, Timbers sat on the tussle of blankets, bedded the shirt-tails safely in her lap and patted a place on the mattress beside her. She sat up straight and wanted the policewoman to do the same so that it would all look ridiculous.

"I was going to ask Ned to come," Miss Hillier said as she stepped properly into the room.

"Good job, you didn't," Timbers said tartly. "We're not speaking."

Jennie looked surprised. "He didn't say."

"That's because he doesn't know. He's seeing someone. I mean, I don't mind. God, it's none of my business. Why should I care? But he could have said."

"Seeing someone? Ned? Don't be ridiculous. Have you seen the state of him?"

"One of the girls said, that's all I'm saying. And I'm saying he could have mentioned it, that's all."

"Timberdick, I've got something to tell you." Carefully, Miss Hillier smoothed her place on the bed and sat down. "The dead man was called Donald Seaton and he was stabbed in the neck, probably while he was sitting on the bank. The doctors say that he couldn't have died in the crash. So he was murdered."

"My God, they've put you in charge of the case, have they?" Do you buy underwear that your mother would like, she wondered. Every bit about you says you've never been undressed, you know that? I mean, you know that's what people think when they look at you?

Jennifer looked straight ahead. She didn't want to look at Timbers when the girl was wearing a man's shirt and nothing else. She said, "I'm not in charge. They've asked me to speak to you, that's all. Because they think I know you."

"Because you've tried to lock me up three times?" (But Miss Hillier had never succeeded, they both acknowledged with a look.)

"Timberdick, I need to get back into C.I.D. This could be my chance, if I get a full statement from you."

"Lots of clues, you mean, so that you can solve someone else's case?"

"Yes. It – doesn't sound very nice."

"Why should it? You never were nice."

"Ned says, you knew Leaper the Porter was lying."

"Bugger 'Ned says'."

"Please."

"He told me I had to get under the carriage because people in the train were going to die. That was rubbish. He told me to bang things like hook-nuts and couplings and backplates – and it all sounded rubbish, even when he was saying it. And when he left me there, the first time, he said he was going for a jack. Where? Where could he get one of those? Then, the second time, he said he was going to speak to the firemen. That's when I found the body."

Jennie listened carefully. "Who did you notice at the scene?" she asked.

"Barbara Bellamy."

Jennie nodded. "D.C. Furrows has already questioned her. He was sure she was hiding something, so I checked up. She used to live in the Seaton's house before he did. He bought the house from her, two years ago. But she didn't mention it in her statement."

"You've told D.C. Furrows about that?"

"No, actually. I haven't."

Timberdick tried to help. "Leaper told me that no-one was in the third carriage."

"Definitely not," Jennie agreed. "It was empty from three stops up the line. And another thing, the train was late. It had been held up by signals at Willersley Halt."

"The girl with the engine driver. She was there. A pretty girl."

Jennie nodded. "Lucy, his daughter. She had been waiting in the car park to take him home."

"The bloke who was with me, though I never saw the going of him."

"I wanted to ask you about him."

"The Man from Scurries. He'd been sniffing around for a couple of weeks, wanting a girl to go with him on a train. Baz Shipley set it up so that we could meet at the top of Moore's Lane at midnight, then he was going to drive me to these disused carriages. He got it all worked out in his head, even down to his fancy dress. When we got into the carriage he changed into these old fashioned holiday clothes. You get it sometimes; a bloke spends months working things out his head and plans it all like a mountain exhibition."

"Expedition."

"Yeah. Me and Baz Shipley think it's to do with the bomb. It's got everyone thinking what they'd do in their last four minutes and blokes up and down the country are working out weird pictures in their heads. Well, Scurries had got it all worked out, except he was late. Ned thinks that means something. Where was he? Why was he late when Baz had fixed it all up, just minutes before."

"I'll speak to Baz about that. She's your friend on the landing, isn't she? The rather attractive girl with long legs?" Then Jennie asked, "Did you see anyone on the railway lines?"

Timbers remembered hearing people before the crash. "Scurries heard them as well. He just said, 'be quiet,' and we got on with things." She shook her head. "It was too dark to see anything clearly. The porter, of course, he could have walked along the track and no one would have noticed."

When Jennie reminded her that Fred Leaper was a hero, she said "Of course," and Jennie said, "Nothing else, then."

"Except the carriages. They weren't the same. The front one was wider than the other two. I remember thinking, that can't be right."

Jennie took some time to absorb the observation. "I don't know about trains," she said lamely.

"You could mention it to the Railway Police."

"Yes, I will." Jennie stood up. "I'll let you get on with things," she said. Then, "Timbers, I'd like us to be better than we are. I mean, I haven't arrested you since Gedling Close and that was years ago."

"One year," Timbers put in. "Last November. One year exactly."

"Not since then. Look, you can't think that I'm out to get you. God, you can't say that. They've stuck me in the Training School, haven't they? I can't get anyone from there. Special responsibility for young women probationers, they say. Huh! I can't even sack them for kissing in the corridors. And they dress as they like. In secret, I mean, not on top. Sometimes, I think-"

"Did you go to boarding school?"

Standing in the middle of the room, Jennie put a sad confessional look on her face. "Why do you ask? Because I'm dowdy?"

"Because you're very girlie." Then, "Sorry, that's rubbish. People say I'm girlie but they don't mean I'm like you." Timbers checked the button at the top of the sailor's shirt. She said, "Look, people think that I grew up in a children's home. They're wrong. I suppose its just as nonsense when I say you went to boarding school."

"Yes, I did," said Jennie suddenly. "I did go to a boarding school. My parents sent me when I was eleven. They wanted to show everyone that they could afford it, I think. You're right. You're thinking that none of the girls liked me and that I got picked on and I'm incredibly shy because of things that happened. Yes, you're right. And I worry sometimes because I sound so like my mother. 'Rather attractive girl with long legs,' I said; just like my mother would've said. Same words. Same voice."

"And you think girls like me are a smell."

Jennie stepped forward to plead, no.

"You do. We've seen it under your nose."

"No."

"You think we're mess on the pavements. You've said it." From now on, I shall call you Jennifer in my head, thought Timbers. Then she laughed to herself. 'Jennifer-in-my-head.' What a good name.

"Not for ages, I haven't. Ned says-"

"And you can bugger Ned as well."

"O.K." No longer prepared to argue, Jennie asked, "Do you know who's seeing him? I mean, I simply can't believe it. Have you seen the state of him recently? Look, it can't be true. Ned and I have known each other for a long time and he would have mentioned it. He trusts me. Look, do you know who?"

"One of the girls said he's seeing one of the others." Timbers shrugged, "It could be anyone."

Jennie thought for a moment. "Listen, here's how we'll find out. Come on, you want to know, don't you?"

"Don't care," said the other child in the playground. "It'd be a giggle, 's'pose."

The merchant seaman barged into the room, laughing over the bundle of bank notes in his hand. "Who's'is?" he said, having elbowed Jennie to one side.

"Police Inspector Hillier," said Timbers. "She used to be CID," she added in a mocking tone. "See-Aye-Dee."

"God," he said and grabbed for the shirt on Timbers shoulders.

"Of course," Timber leaned forward on the bed. "If you want it."

"She's not a policeman," he insisted.

"Well, she's not a tart. Policemen and tarts is all there is up here. You'll not find any other types of women."

"We've not finished yet," he said angrily. "You know that, you cow."

"Shall we ask our detective about that?"

He tried to look menacing with muscles on his torso and his square jaw pumping. "Well, give me back my shirt."

Timbers freed the tails that she had been sitting on then peeled the shirt away like Christmas wrapping. Her large breasts came free and she leaned back to make the most of them. She crossed one leg over the over, not because she was shy of the policewoman but she had learned not to show men things that were out of the question.

"Watch your back, bone-face," he said, stuffing the shirt ends in his trousers. "Just watch where you stand at night, yeah?" Then he noticed Jennie again. "Hey, you want to come downstairs and dance with me." He moved towards her.

"Get off me!" Jennie snapped.

"You a cop? That right?"

"Animal!"

Timbers realised that Jennie was going to get this wrong. She tried to get between them but she was too late.

Jennie kicked out, catching Timbers knee and sending her squealing into the sailor's stomach. He vomited immediately – beer and skittles coming out of his mouth, Timbers said later, like wet popcorn. He regained his breath, threw his head back and roared. His money had flown across the room and he grabbed a head of hair in each hand to stop the girls from getting at it. They screamed with pain. Screamed, louder than they needed and longer, telling the world that things had gone awry.

Baz Shipley was already at the bedroom door. She hallowed like a cowboy in a movie and crashed the china pot over his head. Behind her, a curly haired man, who had paid twelve shillings to see her without any clothes on and thought she was reneging, pulled at her shoulders and they fell back into the passage. Jennie rushed forward. Perhaps she was trying to get away but she tumbled Timbers and the sailor out of the door. She heard Timbers shout, "Get her out!" but there was no chance now. The first floor of the Hoboken Arms had gone wild. Women flew like cats through the air, snatching at any limbs they could reach. Drunken men threw punches in any direction. Booze, shoes, tables and chairs crashed against the walls. Now the fight had started, the rough crowd wanted their bellyful of violence before all the ammo was spent. A girl called Bella, in jeans and no top, wanted to get at Baz Shipley; she trampled over bodies, getting a brown ale bottle from somewhere, and calling for the girl to face her. Then she got her foot trapped and a sweating fat man twisted her long tawny hair round and round one hand and wrenched the bottle from her with the other. Bella threw her head back and started to cry. Fattie got his legs around her waist and mauled her and then two men were on her. Then three. Timbers saw Jen's face come up from the floor. The policewoman didn't seem to know that blood was coming out of one eye. She turned away and saw a girl in a chemise sitting crossed legged at one end of the passage, squealing as two others pulled her hair, making her twirl in a circle on her bottom. A light bulb exploded over the staircase. Someone had told the band to play loudly; the piano and drums thudded through the Public's ceiling to the first floor carpet. Bedroom clocks shuddered along their mantelpieces. Pictures and mirrors fell from the walls. Lampshades slipped from their seating. The Hoboken was jumpin'.

A bedroom window flew open. A woman in a homemade bra stretched out and yelled "Murder!"

"I'll bloody murder you, bitch!" Someone grabbed her head from behind. Then a mains radio, ripped from the wall, shot through the window, crashing to smithereens on the road. Now the fight had gone public. Now, it was a police job; that was the rule.

Worried men were trying to get away; several carried their clothes in bundles before them. Another window smashed and the tough guy bellowed as he jumped. "Bastard!" shouted Timbs, as she crawled to the safety of Room Four. "The bastard's got away with his money." One of the fugitives had broken his leg at the top of the stairs and sat squawking like a fowl with a snapped wing. Chloed was mad in the hallway below. "Bloody cattle," she called. "Like bloody cattle. You need bloody stunning." Suddenly, a man in a dog collar and two girls, made up as nuns in underwear, were in the room with Timbers. The door was locked and one of the girls had the key. Timbers didn't recognise them. The women didn't work for Chloed. The man smiled wickedly. His voice, full of spit, was like a burglar's whisper. "Right, sisters of mercy, time to teach her a lesson." Timbers ripped a table lamp from its socket and got ready.[2]

Police cars outside – brakes and tyres and clanging bells – made matters worse in the corridor. Now, every bit of violence had to be squeezed into the two minutes that remained. Howls went up as the losers tried to mop blood from their faces and out of their hair. The broken legged man shuffled half way down the stairs, then sat still and called everyone 'sir', even the girls. Bella, in tears, crawled into one of the small bedrooms. There, she found Jennie in a cupboard and told her to keep quiet. The fat man armed himself with struts from an iron bedstead and baited the policemen, even before they appeared. Baz made her stand as well. She stood on the top step and threw shoes, bottles and chair legs down the staircase; she was the first to be arrested. Yelling and kicking, she was determined to display everything as they carried her away.

---

[2] I got this story from Timberdick. However, Betty 'Slowly' Barnes has read my manuscript and insists that the vicar and nuns weren't there that night. "They were notorious in 1967 but no-one had heard of them before that. Timbers wants you to tell everyone that she saw them years before anyone else. The little tyke always had to be first in everything." (They didn't get on together.)

Five

A Shot from a Window

Wednesday afternoon in the city and folk in the Goodladies neighbourhood busied themselves with small things. Mrs Manson sat in the concrete bus shelter with her tabby cat on her lap. She waved the double deckers by because she was just sitting, that's all. Cloth-capped Berkeley came out of the newsagents with papers and bread. He hadn't worked for fourteen years and said that he hated women (never mind the nudie books under his bed). In Cardrew Street, 'Old Mother' Shipley swept the broken glass from the pavement in front of her house. The men had brought her Baz back at four in the morning and she was still sleeping upstairs. Ma worried about her. Not because she was on the game – hadn't she been there herself before the last war? But because her grown-up Beryl looked too good. She liked to show off her legs – well, she would – but Baz's legs were long and golden and made her look like a pony. Ma couldn't explain that; just when she walked she made people think of a pony. And Baz was too cocky. Ma had hoped that borstal would knock the arrogance out of the girl but she showed off now as much as she had ever done. She would walk down the street and hold her head up and toss her hair. Ma feared that people would want to bring her down a peg or two.

At half past three, when the back roads were empty, except for the dustmen carrying bins on their shoulders from the back yards to the dustcart, I got Chloed to open the back door of the Hoboken and we talked in her kitchen. Lillie Horsepool, who used to the run the pub, would have sat with me at the wooden table and we would have munched an afternoon breakfast, but Chloed wouldn't stand still. While I sat with a mug of hot tea, she looked into one cupboard, then another, ducked her head under the sink, then marched from room to room. When I asked a question, she called the answer from another part of the pub, then poked her head into the kitchen to explain things further. I managed to tie her down only when curiosity got the better of her and she asked, "What are you doing here?"

"Sit down and I'll tell you," I said. I waited for her to settle on the bench opposite me. "I'm on the sick so I can't go into the police station, but I want to find out about the railway accident. What have people been saying in the pub?"

"They're saying there's going to be trouble in Farringdon Street!" she responded enthusiastically. "Teddy boys and mods and rockers. Greasers and all."

"No, Chloed. Be serious. What have people said about the train crash."

"That Fred Leaper should get an award. And there's been talk of a collection for a plaque."

"Nothing else?"

"Except that you've found a girlfriend."

"That's nonsense," I insisted. "Lord, look at me, Chlo'. What do you think?"

"The girls say that the lady detective is sweet on you. You used to go out, didn't you?"

"Not at all. Good Heavens, I'm over fifty and fat. And Jennie's too young in any case."

Chloed understood. She said, "And she's an Inspector so she wouldn't bother with a lazy Constable." That rankled a little.

Then she wanted to know how Lillie had died. I said that she had killed herself and she said, "I know that. I want to know how."

"The pub got too much for her and there was trouble with the girls. She started to blame herself for things that happened. To Timbers mainly, but the others as well."

"So what did she do?"

"She fell from the railway bridge opposite the Station Road Hotel."

"She fell? She didn't jump?"

"She let herself fall. 'Jump' sounds too dramatic. It wasn't dramatic. Timbers saw it and says it was as quiet as drowning. Slipping beneath the surface for the last time."

"Tell me about her?"

"She came from London after the war."

"No, sorry. I mean Timberdick. Tell me about Timberdick. People say you're her best friend."

But Chloed wouldn't let me talk. She said, "You know, she was in here the other day, going on about how bad the tele was. 'They've taken Lunchbox off, the buggers.' You know how she talks, as if she's sucking on a sponge cake. 'And Emergency Ward's no good any more,' she said. Then she said, why couldn't we have Superintendents like Lockhart is on the tele? I said, Good God girl, he's old enough to be your father. You know who she means, don't you? The man from No Hiding Place."

"He's not, actually."

"He is, every week. With that dishy Sergeant."

"I mean, he's not old enough to be her father. Timbers is thirty four, so Raymond Francis would have to be nearly sixty."

"Well, that's what he is."

"You see, Timbers hasn't met many nice policemen." I got up and walked through to the bars. When she caught up with me, she asked how long I had known her. "Since 1957. She was sleeping on the steps of St Mary's Vestry. But she's been in the city since she ran away from home at 15."

"So she's been a tart for twenty years."

I nodded.

"In the same place."

I shrugged. "Some people move on. Others get stuck." She waited for me say something more, so I added, "She started out waiting for her mother to come looking for her. Her mother never did, so she's still waiting. That's why this baby thing is important to her. She doesn't like kids and wouldn't want one of her own, but she feels responsible for the one on the train. She doesn't want to let it down, like she was." I asked, "There was a fight in here last night?"

"A small one, that's all. Nothing to worry about. Some idiot phoned the police, from one of the houses in the street, I think. She reads you know."

"Of course she can read."

"Of course, I know she can. But I'm saying she does it. A lot of it.

Love stories in the mornings. She's got loads of paperbacks, she says. That makes her sound lonely, doesn't it?"

I didn't want to talk about Timbers' life on her own. I said, "You told Inspector Hillier that a young girl came looking for Timbs in the pub."

She nodded. "About an hour before the fight."

"Can you describe her?"

"I don't know." She considered the picture in her head, then said, "Six-or-seventeen, but it was hard to tell. She was young but mature. And clean. Yes I'd say she was clean, not just the way she looked, but the way she touched things. She came from a good home, that's what I thought. Why are you asking?"

"Black hair, green eyes, skin as white and soft as marshmallow, and a mouth like pink strawberries."

"Yes, that's her. I mean, you make her sound like a cartoon character, painted by numbers. But if you wanted to describe her in a love letter, yes, that's what you'd say. Skin like marshmallow."

"But it's a nasty love letter, Chloe. Mo Tucker has told me that Scurries has been writing rhymes on the dog's toilet wall. About the girl with soft eyes and what he'd like to do to her."

"The dog's toilet?"

"The Gents at the dog track. That's what worried poor Mo on the night Scurries met Timbers."

"Soft eyes? It could be her, but Mo knows more than she's telling. Let's face it, soft eyes is hardly Timbers, is it?" Then, she grabbed hold of my wrist. "You're a policeman. Do you think they'll close me down?"

"What? Because of one fight? I shouldn't think so."

"No, not that. Because I've changed the place. Lillie got up to all sorts of things, but she kept it quiet. I'm loud, Mr Machray. Do you think they're going to say that dirty goings-on are going on?" The tremor in her accent made the repetition sound like the beginning of a song.

I said that I didn't think so. "These are new times, Chloed. Nobody's too sure what ought to be allowed and oughtn't. My guess, they'll leave you alone and see what you can teach them. Don't frighten the horses."

Tired and feeling unsexy, Timberdick was on her way to work. Through the cobbled alleyway between the privies of back-to-back houses, down to the mud and stony patch where nice Mrs Pitt had been trying to grow things for eight years, and across the ashfelt playground of swings and slides. The night was already drawing in but ten year old Stuart Morrison still kicked the scarred leather football against the brick wall. He wore short trousers, long socks pushed down to his lace-up shoes and a heavy grey shirt that had to last all week. The other boys had gone home thirty minutes ago but Master Morrison practised on. The lads had painted white goal posts on the wall and he wanted to be expert at hitting the crossbar. His father had told him that Dixey Dean had been able to do it, sixty times out of sixty, in the olden days. Tonight the light was so poor that he could hardly see the mark but he knew when he hit it and he knew when he missed.

When Timberdick marched, long legged, across the recreation yard, young Morrison caught the ball in two hands and stood and watched. Timbers wore a bright orange miniskirt as thick as a doubled army blanket but so short that it covered her bottom without reaching the tops of her legs. Instead of buttoning her crepe blouse she had tied it in a knot at the front so that her breasts bounced indoors as she walked.

Morrie fingered the football stitching. He didn't love Timbers in the way that he loved Baz Shipley but he still wanted to save his money so that he could do the things to Timbers that his three sisters talked about. He stayed watching until she started along the scrub path beside the chain link fence. Then he kicked the football, extra carelessly, against the old wall. Pointless! What was the point in saving up when he would never know how much she charged?

It was an uneasy night, warm enough for a storm. A stale smelling breeze tried to get up in the back yards and grit from the gutters dirtied the front window sills where they had been built too close to the slabs. Televisions were on in every front room. Some curtains were closed, some were not and Timbers could look in the homes as she passed. Streets away, someone kicked some glass bottles and girls squealed as they ran away from the boys. Timbers was slopping her sandals along the pavements, not fifty yards from Goodladies Road, when she was caught by a voice in the shadows.

"Here. Hold up." Fred Leaper was hiding in an archway between two terraced houses. "You want to give me a few minutes."

Not really, thought Timberdick. You're ugly like an old frog with fish fins for a moustache. She could taste how they would smell, close up. But he'd be short lived, she thought. She knew what to do with old codgers like Leaper; take their money and embarrass them so that they want it over and done with.

"Oh no," he said, quick to put her right. "I want to talk, that's all. Look, I couldn't help it. You – you want to come in here?"

Timber went with him, away from the light of the street and into a nook of dustbins and old hose reels.

"Like I say, I couldn't help it. I know you saved those people. I saw it. And that's what I said to people at first. But talk got around so quickly."

Timbers said that it didn't matter. People didn't want her to be a hero. She pushed her back against the wall, kept her hands out of the way and made him think about her body. They were so close in this tiny alcove that he had to think about it. He couldn't help it.

"You were with Scurries, weren't you?"

"Is that his name?"

"Oh yes. He's been hanging around the terminus for weeks." He smiled all the time he spoke, like he wanted to be her uncle.

"You couldn't find him for me?" she asked. "He's not been back to his shop, they say."

"If that's what you want, my dear. I'll ask around the lads."

When Timbers didn't say anything, Leaper said "Yes," and wrapped his nose in the palm of his hand. And 'Yes' again. Excited.

"You want to have me, don't you?" she said, knowing that he hadn't decided yet and needed a push.

"Oh, no. At least, not here. Perhaps in a different place. Your place, perhaps. I'll come round one day."

Bugger off. You're not getting my address.

"Why'd you kill him, Mr Leaper?"

Leaper was appalled. "I didn't murder him! Good Lord, don't go saying things like that. People are saying enough about me without you putting ideas in their heads."

"The murder was done while I was under the carriage. I saw Seaton on the bank – and then I saw him dead at my feet. You were closest to him during that time."

"I didn't kill him!"

"Who else was about, Mr Leaper? We heard people on the track, a few minutes before the crash."

"No-one, as I said. You'd have to ask Luce. She'd have seen more than both of us. She was in the car, waiting to take her father home. Lord, you heard people on the track, you're saying? People who could have derailed the train? You think it was done on purpose?"

Timbers nodded. "You've done, have you?"

"What?"

"Have you finished talking? I mean, you've said all you wanted to say?"

"If you say so. God, you're a rude little cow, aren't you? Weren't you listening when your mum spoke about manners?"

"I've got to work, Mr Leaper."

"Fred," he said, without expression. "Call me, Fred."

"I thought you were cross with me, for being rude?"

He dug into his trousers. "Yes, well. Look, there is something I like. I'm on my own, you know that. You'd understand that?" He pressed some loose change into her hand. "Here's a round of drinks. To be friendly, yeah? And perhaps I'll come round to your's, one day, eh? One day soon?"

Timberdick realised that he wasn't going to give her any more money that night so she did nothing to keep him. He got ready to leave, straightening his windcheater on his shoulders, and he stepped away from her. "You understand," he said. (People always knew that Timbers understood what they did to her.) She watched him cross the road and amble along the far pavement with the bumbling gait of an overweight, sore legged old man who should have stayed at home. She watched his figure disappear into the shadows of the dusk.

She walked to the junction of Goodladies Road. Some people would have recognised her footsteps as she sauntered lazily, almost cheekily, past their front windows. Upstairs, some of the young people in bed would grow up with the sound of her walking at night being a memory of their childhood and home. Folk around here were used to seeing her every night, sometimes at lunchtimes and sometimes even in the early mornings. She had been on the corner of Goodladies Road, where three roads meet at the Hoboken Arms, for so many years that she knew every bump and crack beneath her feet. She knew where to stand, where not to look. She knew the light and shade, the draughts and the odours from the alehouse. When she heard a noise, she knew the street it was in and whether it was coming or going. She could see a car turning in from a side road and say if it was getting ready to stop or merely slowing down for a look.

She stood near the front step of Number 152, folded her arms across her stomach and shivered. Tired and unsexy and wanting to do nothing. Headlights caught her but she didn't step forward; they were going too fast. Then a car slowed and the man leaned across to look but shook his head. He thought she was too old, too thin, too gawky. Timberdick felt as humiliated now as she had on her first night, eighteen years ago. The feeling never got better. The man had looked and decided that he could do better elsewhere. Perhaps he had used her before and knew that she was cold and bony. 'God, your bum's like it's been in a fridge,' someone had told her before last Christmas. Still, she laughed when she thought about it. 'What do you do?' he had asked. 'Stick it in a fridge before you come out?' At least, he didn't call her Goose Face; she hated that.

A lonely-looking man, darkly dressed and furtive, appeared at a street corner, a hundred yards away. She couldn't make out his face but she hoped he was the driver of a car that had passed by ten minutes before. He had looked a timid sort, easy money, not given to much adventure. Probably, he had parked on the quiet forecourt of Smithers Motors so that he could walk back discreetly. Some men preferred her not to see their cars, as if she was collecting numbers or likely to snatch their keys. More often, they couldn't trust their wives or mothers not to detect that another girl had been in the front seat. You're safer with the ones that worried, Timbers thought. She stepped forward so that the yellow streetlight caught the profile of her chest as she turned a little away from him. She couldn't help that it also showed her sparrow's legs and knobbly shoulders. She wobbled her knees, just once or twice, so that they wobbled her bottom. And she turned again, throwing back her head to encourage him.

Then, as he crossed the street, she recognised his weathered face. "Bloody Scurries," she muttered and thought about walking off. "He's got a bloody nerve."

"Please!" he shouted, sensing her hesitation.

So he wants a bloody row, does he? She stepped to the kerb and was ready to shout something horrible – but things got in the way.

First, she heard a windowpane crack behind her and Mrs Horsley leapt from her armchair, shouting 'bleddy sods!' Then she heard a second crack, from across the road and high up, and a metal pellet bouncing of the tin littler can on the lamp-post. Timberdick screamed. She covered her face and crumpled to the ground. She crouched like a hedgehog and went on screaming, slapping the tops of her feet against the pavement. Like a child in a tantrum.

Scurries' sweaty hands were on her back and shoulders and Mrs Horsley was outside with her front door open. "Is the poor slut shot?"

"From the pub. From the staircase window," he said, red-faced and out of breath. "Can we get her inside?"

"Not in my house, my man," said the woman from Number 152. "I can't have a girl like her in my house. No matter what."

People were running from the Hoboken Arms. "We've lost her!"

"I saw her, though!"

"A young lass! Not more than eighteen and an airgun."

Scurries bent his head low. "I can't wait, Timbers," he whispered. He had peppermint breath and smelt of scent. "You see that? I can't be caught here, can I? But the train, Timbers, it was a tadpole. Tell the police it was a tadpole. Timbs, I think it's important."

"Grab him!" she shouted.

But no-one took any notice.

"Don't let him get away!"

Scurries was already fifty yards away, running along the pavements in his Fat-Mouse way.

"It wasn't him, dearie," said old Mrs Horsley as she helped Timbers sit up. Mr Horsley was bringing some water, she said. "It was a girl. You're gentleman will get her. Let's hope so."

But Timbers knew that would make things worse.

PART TWO

THURSDAY AND FRIDAY

Six

A First Chapter of Witnesses

Timberdick slept in my bed while I drew an armchair to the hearth and dozed with my woollen socks too near to the gas fire. When I looked in at two, she was still crying with her face buried between the pillow and the mattress and the blankets drawn over her head. But I checked again at half past three and she was asleep. I left Dogberry to look after her. (He's the caricature of an old watchman who sits on the face of my bedside clock. We don't make good policemen in the ordinary way, Dogberry and I, so that made the clock one of my favourite knick-knacks.)

I didn't want to sleep deeply. I wanted to listen for any sound of Timbers stirring but I had set my Decca portable at a low volume and the foreign lady speaking between last year's records soon sent me off. The next thing I heard was Timbers making noises on the stove.

I had slept in my trousers with the waist and flies open, and my copper's heavy cloak covering me like a blanket. I got myself together and shuffled through to the kitchen.

"I'm cooking breakfast," she said, meaning that she didn't want to talk about the shooting. "Three poached eggs and pepper. You're out of bread so there's no toast." She was wearing my pyjamas top as a nightie and she had my uniform socks on her feet. The socks were thick enough to go inside my patrol boots. I smiled at the picture she made.

I leaned against the draining board. "You can't go back home and you can't stand on the streets. It's too dangerous."

"Have you found my baby yet?" she asked, full of accusation.

"You know I haven't."

"Have you done anything about it?"

"Bits"

61

"What?"

"I've spoken to Chloed."

"Chloed! Chloed? What would she know about it? God, you're useless."

"Timbers, never mind the baby. Someone tried to kill you last night because you were too close to the murder on the train."

She turned away from the stove and slid three fried eggs onto the plate I was already holding.

She saw me thinking 'poached?'

"I said you like three poached eggs. I can't do them poached, so you've got them fried. And no-one tried to kill me. It was an air pistol, Ned. They wanted to scare me, that's all. Do your own pepper."

She walked off to the sittingroom while I stayed in the kitchen and made two mugs of tea. I had finished eating the eggs before the water boiled. When I joined her in front of the fire, she was sitting on a rocking chair with her legs up, her bare feet on the seat and her knobbly knees either side of her chin. My pyjamas top drowned her, but her position still meant that too much was uncovered. She wasn't showing off; I had seen her naked so many times that her rudeness wasn't remarkable.

"They didn't shoot at me because I was a witness," she said. "That wouldn't make sense. Seaton was murdered while I was under the train and there was too much chaos for me to notice anything that the killer would want to hide. No, I have been thinking about this. The gun-girl wants revenge; she thinks that I'm responsible for his murder because she saw me coming from the coach where the baby was. That's what this is all about, Ned. She was Seaton's lover."

"If that's true. We'd better find the real killer before the gun-girl tries to shoot you again." I said, "Cover yourself up, Timbs."

"Sorry." She pushed the hem of my pyjamas between her thighs – which did no good at all. "Lord, what I have got the girl into?"

"Don't be stupid."

"Scurries ran after her. What if he gets hold of her? And she's just a teenager, people said."

"You're not making sense, Timbers."

"I left that baby on the train and now the girl who shot me is mixed up with Scurries. If I hadn't been there-"

"That's stupid. You can't go around saying, 'If I wasn't there.'"

She leaned forward and buried her face in her hands. When it surfaced, drawn and washed out, she said, "I feel that I'm in the middle and the world's falling in on me. It's like I'm collapsing in on myself."

"I know," I said quietly.

"I'm frightened to go to sleep, Ned. Every time I close my eyes I can smell the oil and cinders from the train. I can see metal bits wanting to bite me."

"You've got to-"

"Don't tell me what to do. It's all right for you, but-"

"Look, but nothing, pet." I turned my back on her, looked along the mantelpiece for my pipe, then cursed because my tobacco pouch wasn't with it.

"I've got to sort it out," she insisted.

"That's stupid."

"I'm not stupid," she snapped.

"It is. It's stupid." Wanting to explain.

She got out of her chair and stepped towards me. "It's not!"

"It is."

She went to slap my face but I stopped her.

She said, while I held her wrist, "I'm going to sort it out. Are you going to help me?"

"Of course," I said and let her go.

"I want to speak with Barbara Bellamy. She's the person I know best on the train."

"Shouldn't we do that together?"

"No, because you're going to find Lucy Lamey, the engine driver's daughter. She came to meet him just after the crash, so she must have seen someone running from the scene."

"And her dad, of course."

Timbers nodded. "I want to ask him about tadpoles."

"Tadpoles?"

"And why the train was stopped by signals at Willersley Halt."

"Wouldn't Fred Leaper know that?" I asked.

"Oh, I do want to speak with Mr Leaper. Like bloody definitely, I do."

I started to the bedroom for some clean clothes. When I got to the door, she said, "I can do it, Ned. I'm all right."

I turned to answer her. "I'm not sure I can keep up. I don't know what I've got inside to offer you."

"I'm sorry that I tried to hit you. I've wanted to fight everyone since the crash."

* * *

Bellamy's homely haberdashery was a little thin shop on the Nore Road. The Number Two bus stopped outside, so there was usually a queue of housewives ready to look at the bobbins, ribbons and babies' bibs in the window. When Barbara Bellamy wasn't behind the counter – because the shop was very often quiet – she could be found in the florist's across the street, or next door with the hairdresser. Babs liked to chat and usually had much to contribute. Mr Fawn had to be more careful with the butcher's lass now that Babs had put the word about. And she was asking questions about Mrs Fawn's Tuesdays off. Had they got anything to do with the package that Babs had seen in the woman's saddlebag? Cartons of wine from a shop in Winchester. What was Mrs Fawn doing in card shops when everyone knew that she had no family? Canny folk let Barbara Bellamy's gossip pass by; generally there was nothing to come of it. But the Fawn woman had already said that the talk ought to be sorted on the front street. Mr Fawn had things to say too. For a start, why was Barbara Bellamy spending nights in her shop? The confrontation was expected daily.

Timbers walked up the Nore Road in the rain. A mother and child were sheltering in Bellamy's doorway, the infant leaning forward in his pushchair so that he could press fingerprints on the windowpane. When Timbers approached, the mother told him off and withdrew from Timbers' path.

The bell above the door rang on its spring as she walked in and Timbers, not saying a word, locked the door behind her and pulled down the blind.

"What the-!"

But Timbers marched past the shopkeeper, turned left at the end of the narrow passage and stamped up the staircase.

"You can't-!"

Barbara Bellamy put the cotton reels back in the tray, slammed shut the drawer and started after the trespasser. "Just who do you think you are!"

"I'm Timbers." She was sitting on the top step, picking at a chip of dried skin on her knee. "And I want to know what you've told the police."

Babs stopped half way up. "What?"

"You lived in the dead man's house before he did. Have you told them?"

"I made a statement," she replied, keeping still. "We all did. Lucy, Fred and me. There were no other passengers, except Donald. And he didn't, of course."

"Didn't?"

"Make a statement."

"But you didn't mention the same address?"

"Look, we can't talk about it like this while you're blocking my way and-" She shook her fingers irritably. "Thingy. Scratching your knees."

They went to the stock room overlooking the bus stop. For twenty minutes the two women stepped around the packing cases, coats on runners, old shop tackle and spent stationery – they moved carefully, like chess pieces, each determined to checkmate the other by stealth. Babs had more money, more clothes, better shoes and smoother legs (though Timbers noticed that she wore thicker nylons than should have been necessary) but she would have died for Timbers' breasts. And Timbers let her know it with every pose she struck.

"I know you," Babs said. "Ye-es, I do."

"I don't think so," said Timbers and sat on the windowsill, knowing that this Bellamy woman wouldn't want to show herself to the street below.

"You were there, too."

"Yes."

"But no, that's not it." Barbara Bellamy fixed her eyes on Timbers' face and glided forward, her feet light on the bare wood floorboards. "Last year you came with a chubby one. Long black hair and round faced. You kept yourself between us while she pinched bracelets from the stand."

Yes, she had visited the shop with Betty 'Slowly' Barnes, but she didn't know the woman had shoplifted. "Bloody liar. And what's it got to do with your lies to the police."

Babs collected a coat hanger. "You thieving tart!" she said as she came forward. She threatened Timbers with the hanger, not seriously but sufficiently to make Timbers steps backwards, dislodging the lid of a cardboard crate.

"What's this? Expensive corsets in Bellamy's?"

"Don't! Please don't pull them out of the box; the man won't take them if they've been thumbed. He's very particular. Mrs Timberdick, they're a special order. Corsets for men."

"These?" Timbers didn't pull them from the carton but she could see that they were white and lacy; too dainty for any man.

"I have to get them made especially. He buys a dozen at a time but wears them only once, then throws them away. He's often my best customer of the month. I couldn't manage without him. Please, don't interfere."

Timbers accused her. "You knew Donald Seaton was on the train."

"No. Come on, he was in the front carriage and there was no communicating door. How would I know? Even at the hospital, I didn't know. Not until the police told me the morning after."

"But you started the journey at the same time. You must have seen each other on the platform."

"Look, we'd have sat together, wouldn't we?"

* * *

They were digging up Turks Road again and the kids were playing cricket because traffic was barred. I had walked from the city centre and wanted to use Turks as a short cut to the foreshore of the yacht harbour. But I walked in on a dispute over a high ball. The kids had made a rule that any player who sent a ball to window height should forfeit their wicket (if a batsman) or six (if a bowler). The argument was testy and the leader of the crowd – a ten-year-old girl with the shoulders of a washerwoman – saw the wisdom of seeking adjudication. At first, I was happy to go with the majority, until I saw a look of unfairness on skinny Cheryl's face. She would cry before giving up her bat on such a ruling. I said that I thought the ball had been wide from the start and should be replayed. This was nonsense because everyone knew that I hadn't witnessed the bowling. But the kids were quick to recognise my offering as a solution to an argument that had been going on for too long and, right or wrong, was holding up play. Voices counselled the bowler that getting an 'out' because of a high ball wasn't a worthy wicket because 'high balls' wasn't a proper rule of cricket. "They don't play it at Lords," said a scruff with long socks round his ankles and his hands in the pockets of his short trousers. "Ask anyone as knows."

"Where are you going, Mister?" asked one called Susan.

"The huts on the foreshore."

"Me and Bren will show you a quick way. It's through Donna's back yard and across the scrubland. She's my other sister, Brenda is. Aren't you, little Brendie?"

Play resumed as the girls took me through a gate between two terraced houses.

We were on the seashore within a couple of minutes. It was a cold day and a strong breeze rippled the surface of the grey water. Fifty yards out, dinghies and little yachts bobbed about and righted themselves to the wind. The girls stayed on the bank of rough grass and threw pebbles while I trudged along the stony path to the huts beside the disused railway line.

The engine driver's daughter was wearing overalls and army boots when I found her. She was leaning over the open bonnet of her sportscar with a selection of spanners on the fender. The car had been pushed forward from the old railway hut and stood on the stony ground of the beach path. A transistor radio was playing in the hut. As I approached, I heard a Radio Caroline jingle. She straightened her back and, as foolishly as all mechanics, she wiped an oily rag across her forehead. "The little charmer said I should expect you."

I didn't know what she meant. I said it was a very cold day, hoping she would offer some tea. Instead, she asked about Timbers.

"She's a little shaken up. The pellet didn't hit her."

"She's having a rough week, our Timberdick. First the train crash, then the Hoboken rough house. Now, being shot at."

"You know her?"

"I know she was with Scurries. He's spoken about her."

Lucy Lamey was nineteen, no older, with a supple figure and blonde hair that she tied loosely behind her. She had that happy knack of seeming not to know how attractive she was. She was a careful girl; she thought before she said anything and looked seriously at me.

"Nice car," I said.

"Riley, one-point-five, roadster. Over twelve years old but it's been seen to."

"Yours?"

"An old boyfriend bought it for me. He said he loved me and I said show me how much." She chuckled at her flippancy; of course, it hadn't really happened that way.

"I'm surprised you keep it so close to the sea. I wouldn't have thought the salt was good for it."

"I didn't choose the garage. Dad fixed it up while I was away. And it's the best we could do. He gets it cheap, being the railway's hut."

"Full of surprises, then. Your Dad and your fellow."

She laughed again. "He's not my fellow anymore. The car's better than the bloke, believe me. We could take it for a run, if you like. We could race it up to Willersley Halt and see if I had time to murder a man and get back to the terminus before Dad's train."

"Why would you want to?"

"Murder him? I wouldn't. I didn't even know the bloke. Didn't know his name, until this morning. But 'Charmer' said you'd want to speak to me about it. She said that you'd think I could have done it that way."

"Charmer?"

"The girl who shot Timberdick. Scurries has got her. They were down here this morning."

"What's her real name, Lucy?"

She said, "Cynthia Seaton. I didn't know that she was the dead man's daughter. I'm sorry. Perhaps I should have taken her more seriously." The wind was blowing; she caught her hair and tucked it into the collar of her overalls. I heard the two little girls shouting as they ran away from the beach.

"And you know Scurries?"

"He used to spend a lot of time down by the station. If I was there, we'd share a pot of tea in the café."

"Did he ever mention Mr Seaton to you?"

"Not at all."

"Did you know he was on the line, that night?"

"Not really. But I wasn't surprised when people told me." She waited, then decided that I should know, "Actually, he had asked me to meet him in the railway carriages at night. It was something he'd always thought about. I said I wouldn't and he said he felt bad about asking. That's when he told me about Timberdick. Other girls had spoken to him about her, but he'd looked at her and she wasn't pretty enough for him, he said." She shrugged her shoulders. "He ended up with no other choice, I guess."

I asked if she had seen Timbers on the night of the train crash.

"I was waiting for Dad at the front entrance. If Scurries and Timberdick were on the disused line, I wouldn't have seen them. Constable, I was there from twenty to one until three in the morning. Cynthia will tell you the same. She thought I was her father's lover and she was trying to catch us out. That's what she's saying now. She'd got it wrong, but she was there and she's my alibi. You see, I wouldn't have had time to get up to Wilsea Halt and back. No, I didn't murder Cynthia Seaton's father."

I took my time walking home. I wanted to get my thoughts straight. Scurries and Seaton's daughter were working together. The daughter had been there at the time of the murder. She had suspected Lucy of being her father's lover. Now, perhaps, she suspected Timberdick and that's why she had taken a shot at her.

Light started to fade at half past four. By the time I got home, I was cold and my feet were aching. I closed the curtains, made a cup of tea and was about to nap on the sofa when the phone rang.

"Ned, have you heard about the riot?" It was Jennie.

"Riot?"

"A riot, Ned." She was short of breath. "Have you heard about it?"

"A riot."

"Ned, has anyone said there's going to be a riot?" She was trying to be patient with me.

"Has anyone said?" I played back to her, puzzled.

"God, you're useless," she said and slammed the phone down.

I pulled off my boots, loosened my trousers and lay down in front of the fire. A couple of hours, that's all I wanted. Timbers will be all right with Leaper the Porter. She'd come to no harm with him.

* * *

Fred Leaper opened his front door at eight o'clock and said, "I wasn't sure you'd come," as if they were lovers meeting in secret. He was scrubbed up, freshly groomed and ready for her. His face was a shiny pink and his black hair was damp from a wash. He looked like a boarding school boy in his Sunday best. He took her coat, very politely, and showed her to an easy chair where she could keep warm by the gas fire while he brewed a pot of tea in the kitchen. Timberdick noticed the treats laid out on a corner table. There was strawberry jam in a patterned glass dish attended by home baked scones. Whipped cream stood up in two saucers and a huge cake was so laden with soft chocolate icing that the sponge had begun to sink in the middle.

"You started me thinking, yes you did," he called through, but Timbers didn't want to listen. She thought, a man lives alone in these rooms. He had filled it with pictures – of places, not people – and trinkets that meant nothing to others. He wants it to feel like his mother's old house, she thought, but she was wrong. For years, Fred Leaper had fancied a level crossing cottage or a gardener's lodge in a wayside station. Both these notions were a hundred miles from a terraced house in the middle streets of the city. She saw the bookcase and thought he was a great reader but she was mistaken again. Fred had joined the Companion Book Club on his fiftieth birthday and a new volume arrived each month. They were uniform with matching dustwrappers and the same height and, although some had been dipped into, none had been finished. Fred Leaper liked assemblies and timetables and lodging a new book in a line on a bookcase was a task completed in a perpetual schedule. It was a satisfaction unique and unexplained.

He came to the kitchen door. "I've been thinking about it since last night."

Timbers cut in. "You want us to play together."

He nodded. "I've tucked some ten bob notes in an old wage

70

packet behind the clock."

She leant forward and collected the envelop from the mantelpiece. He waited while her spindly fingers counted the money. He was offering more than twice her usual fee, he knew that. He had asked questions on the street before inviting her here.

"I don't do spanking," she cautioned. "Or any tying up."

He faltered. "No, no. I want nothing like that."

The kettle's whistle called him back to the kitchen and Timberdick counted the money again.

"You see, so much of my life's alone. I don't mean living here or fishing. That's treasure. But at work, I'm on my own a lot of the time. And what starts as a word or two in my head gets bigger and more complicated and needs dressing up and more thinking about. Then before I know it, it's the only thing in my head. It steals from me. It steals my time and all of my ideas. And I know that I have to get rid of it. I've got to do it. I've got to spend it. It's like spending money from my pocket. It's like-" relieving myself with a pee, he thought but he didn't say it. "It's like-"

But Timbers didn't want to know what it was like. She couldn't stomach one more sorry tale from a maudlin male with broken bits. Couldn't these men see that the reasons, the excuses and all of the stories were the same? They blamed their mothers, their school and the way people looked at them. Things they had seen and things they had heard before they knew what they meant. They blamed peep shows and images and accidents and unfairness. For half of her life, Timbers had heard nothing different and nothing new. She heard him stir the teapot and waited for him to arrive with everything on a tray.

She said, "You don't have to tell me. Going with me means that you don't have to explain and I don't have to understand. That's what it's about. Doing me means nothing, so who wants to know why?"

Fred Leaper was dithering and biting his lip. The fireplace clock chimed eight thirty and Timbers wanted to be on the slabs by ten. "Look, shall I undress?" she asked, still sitting in the chair but unbuttoning her blouse. "Would that help? Do you want me to take my clothes off?"

He made a noise that meant yes. He was standing at the corner table now and looking into the cups as he poured. "Keep your pants on," he said, very quietly. "I want you to stand up in them."

Timbers gave a phoney smile and stretched to her feet. "Ah, you want to do me in my knickers. I had a Police Super who liked that." Standing in the middle of the carpet, she discarded the blouse and unzipped her skirt so that it fell in a circle about her shoes. She had practised the next movement so that when her hands reached behind to unclip her bra, she made herself stand like a statue that had arisen from the puddle of cloth at her feet.

"Oh, Goodness me, wait!" he said in a hurry. "I must get the music on; that's quite important." Giving Timbers no more than a glance, he went to his Gerrard Radiogram, and set a 45 on the turntable. "Please, I'll be with you in a moment," he said. "I stole it from Seaton. He was dead of course, so he wouldn't have minded. Actually, I'm sure he would have expected it. It's what collectors want, you see, their special items to move on to the next enthusiast. I'm not a real enthusiast, you understand – Ted Heath and Jack Parnell, that's about all I can cope with. But I do like curiosities and this record looked a bit extraordinary. I know enough to take care of Mr Seaton's record for him."

Timbers revealed her breasts and prayed he would stop talking. She felt chilly. Only months ago she could stand for hours with no clothes on but, just recently, she found herself wanting something warm – a shawl or a smock – around her shoulders. The music had started. It sounded like a small jazz band playing far away. The record hissed throughout. She breathed in and bore it – the music and the cold.

"It's awful," said Timbers. "No-one could like this."

"It's a seven inch extended play on a French label I've never heard of."

Timbers closed her eyes and thought, 'Oh God, he's going to explain it to me.'

"I've got to say, it looks cheap. The record's label is coarse and faded and, look, the sleeve's poorly printed on cheap paper."

Timbers looked. The cover showed an eight-piece band, all female, playing at a supper club. She held one corner lightly between a thumb and a finger, as if liking it might be catching.

He said, as he walked back to the tea table, "I can't make head nor tail of the writing but the record's called 'The Ladies Jazz Orchestra at the Metropol Restaurant 1935 and 6.' The singer's a blonde called Vera."

"Yes, I can see that."

"It's a Russian jazz band," he said. "I don't know anything about them"

That's a mercy, she thought.[3]

Fred Leaper left the teacups on the table, picked up the chocolate cake and stepped towards her. "Here now, I want you to hold the sleeve up as if you are reading it but stay standing just as you are." He positioned her hand as artists do to models. "And, and, close your eyes."

"You want me to read with my eyes shut?"

"Yes, yes, it's the tableau that's important, you see. The picture you make."

Another man with pictures in his head! First, Scurries wanted to make love to her on a train while he was dressed like an apprentice at Blackpool. Now, the railway porter wanted to hear music playing as she stood in her pants.

It's because of the bomb, Timbers reminded herself. When folk thought that the world was going to end because of missiles in Cuba, they had asked what their friends would like to do in their last four minutes on earth. It seemed that half the grown-up men in England had kept those images in their heads and wanted Timberdick Woodcock to bring them to life. She promised to mention the theory to Ned Machray, the next time he wanted to be boring. (She also wanted to know if he liked to wear white corsets. After all, he seemed to know a lot about Barbara Bellamy. Perhaps she was his secret lover.)

---

[3]Fifteen years later, I did some leg-work to help my son investigate the disappearance of a young Russian. I spoke to the family about Vera Dmitrievna Dneprova and her All Girl Jazz Band. They researched the story, as best they could, and confirmed that she had worked at the Metropol Restaurant from 1934. She had an affair with an American diplomat, they said. She was arrested on 15 December 1937 – "That is seven years exactly before your Glenn Miller disappeared," they said – and she was sentenced to ten years hard labour. Word gets round. A month later, a widow from Illinois sent me more photo's of Vera, taken on a tour of the Black Sea in 1935. She wanted to buy the record but I said no. By that time, Slowly had grown quite fond of the tunes.

"It took less than a minute for that train to come off the line. Just think if that minute had been different. The engine driver would have taken over my night duty and I would have gone home. In bed and asleep by half past one, I would have been. You would have finished your woe-be-gones with your customer and, I don't know, got on with your life. Donald Seaton, of course, he'd still be dead, murdered, but no-one would have shot you in the street. Please, keep your hand in the air," he reminded her and sat down at her feet with the chocolate cake at his side. "And close your eyes."

"What's a tadpole?" she asked.

He looked no higher than her legs. "Have you closed your eyes?"

"Closed tight," she assured him. "And I'm holding Vera up to my face."

"Yes." He said, steadying his breathing. "Not too close. As if you are admiring her."

But she couldn't feel or hear him doing anything. She wondered if he was worshipping her. Perhaps he longed to look at her feet. Was that it? "What's a tadpole?" she asked again.

"Yes, carry on talking. That's nice."

"Scurries said it to me after I was shot. He said the train was a tadpole. It was important, he said. I should tell the police."

"Yes," he said. "Tell the police." Then she felt him pull at the front of her pants, opening them at the top. He dug his fingers into the soggy cake and they came out with a handful of chocolate cream and sponge. "A tadpole," he said, "is a train with a front coach wider than the others." And he pushed the chocolate mess down the front of her knickers. "Yes, just a little wider-" and Timbers responded before she realised he was describing a tadpole, not asking for more room, "-but enough to make it look like a tadpole." He delivered a second handful and, carefully, almost gentlemanly, pressed the knickers flat against her skin so that the cake crumbs and icing squashed everywhere. "Was the 00:47 a tadpole? Well, you know, I think it might have been." Then he crawled to her backside; this time two handfuls – half the cake in one go – were pushed down the seat of her pants. And more. "Talk to me," he said. "We said that you'd carry on talking." Soon, there was more chocolate cake than her briefs could hold and the sauce started to run down her legs.

"I know a policeman who'd like this record. He goes for odd-ball stuff."

"Yes, well." He was rubbing his palm in circles over the seat of her pants, rubbing the chocolate into her buttocks like make-up on her face. "Of course, he can borrow it, but you must bring it with you whenever you come and see me."

Oh bugger, was she supposed to call again? Bugger, the things a girl has to put up with.

"I want to clean you up," he said, crawling around her. "Leave your knickers when you go. I want to wash them for you and parcel them up, nice and neat."

Ten minutes later, when he was wiping her legs with Scotties, she checked the time again. "I want to be at the Methodist Rooms at half past nine," she said. "Someone looks for me there, sometimes on Thursdays."

"You're not frightened?"

"Of the girl with the gun? No, she won't try again."

"No, I mean the gangs. The gangs that were out last night."

But Timberdick knew nothing of any gangs.

"You shouldn't be out on nights like this."

She laughed. "Nights like this are all I have."

Seven

Learned at Mothers' Knees

The affair of hard beans at Tug Wilson's began with a complaint so quietly made that the cook did not hear of it until he closed at midnight. Little Peter Peers, a pensioner in a white shirt and an old suit, took lunch every day in the snack bar and, more often than not, came back for tea at half past three. 'The old fool,' said folk in the sitting-grooms of the Oakwood Estate and on the doorsteps. Didn't he know that Wilson's was a greasers' café for ton-up boys and their leather clad girlfriends? No-one over 30 should go there, unless they didn't wash and could tell stories of beatniks. But the gossips were wrong. True, the café was the bikers' territory and they enjoyed making outsiders uncomfortable, but Peter was an old man who had taken their teasing and now they looked kindly upon him.

Young Desmond Hawthorn wasn't in the café when Pete mentioned that his baked beans were hard, but the bossy college kid was ready with an opinion when word reached him. 'It's the Spanish,' he asserted. Everyone knows, he said, that the cafes were working a cartel and bought contraband food from the docks. And the Spanish – although it might have been the French – were trying to squeeze every last penny from the trade. And that led to hard beans on Pete's plate.

Hawthorn wasn't an educated teenager but he knew just enough to feign authority when delivering his dissertations to the ton-up youths at Tug Wilson's café. He explained the Common Market debate. He explained the perils of the IMF. And when he emphasised the need to maintain the economies of the Commonwealth, he made it sound as if the hard beans had been put on Pete's plate to imperil the Empire. (He didn't say that, of course. He never mentioned the Empire, he insisted later.)

As for Pete's plate – well, that was quickly settled. Julie (she was out-front while Tug was watching the racing) served up a double plated breakfast in compensation and Tug took Pete home for tea the next day. However, Desmond Hawthorn's propaganda had already got out of hand. On Wednesday evening, a group of youngsters (witnesses said they were not more than thirteen years old) toured the streets behind the Hoboken looking for continental things to break. They didn't find anything but they sounded bad – and they carried clubs. On Thursday evening, Sean from the record shop phoned while I was napping and shouted that he had been told to take Django Rheinhardt out of the window. I told him to do so. These things last for only a few days, I said, and we would deal with the petit gangsters when the fuss had died down.

I telephoned the Duty Sergeant. "Jennie has already been moaning on about this," he sighed impatiently. "I've told the on-call D.C. and he says it's all nonsense. He could believe it if these lads were anti-American or against the commies. But anti-European? Come on, Ned."

"Who's on?"

"Furrows. He says, who cares what the French do to our beans? Listen, you're supposed to be on sick leave, Ned. Go back to bed."

I dressed and went down to the record shop. As I passed the tobacconist, Rennie Tegg reported that a window had been broken in Farringdon Street. "They say that Italians had lived there before Mrs Goudenough. They say she shouldn't have brought the place from Italians. It's like giving them money."

"Call the police station, Rennie"

"It's like things were at the start of the war, before we all learned that we were in it together. It can get bad, Mr Machray."[4]

But when I got to the record shop, the boys immediately sent me to the Stretton Railway Bridge. "Some of the bikers from Tug's have decided that things are getting out of control. They want to face the troublemakers down."

---

[4]I don't know if Rennie made the telephone call. There is no record of the Farringdon Street damage in the police records. When I asked why none of these incidents had been logged, I was told that none had been formally reported. "There has to be a complainant, Machray, you know that."

I had been walking for twenty minutes and I was puffed up and out of breath, but I pressed on. Across the non-conformist graveyard and up the hill to the new traffic lights. I was walking too fast, I knew that. The pump in my chest was working too hard and my head couldn't keep things in shape. I went through dizzy spells and I saw things in a warped way. I had that feeling of being on the edge of something dire; that people I saw were close to losing their balance. Not just the warmongers but ordinary people pushing prams along the pavements and children scuttling along the kerbstones. I saw P.C. Heron across the road from the cemetery gates but I didn't stop to tell him the story. I raised a hand and nodded my big head on my fat shoulders and kept going.

I didn't know that the 13 year olds were campaigning in the opposite direction, about a quarter of a mile to my left. They were looking for French or Spanish prizes again. They had added Italy to their list because of the incident on Farringdon Street and there was talk of Genoa being a bad country too. They kicked and clattered their way through the dustbins at the back of the Cherry Street shops and were half way up the cobbled alley when they found what they were looking for.

Timbers was soliciting by the Methodist porch.

"A French Tart!" trumpeted the subaltern-in-charge

Suddenly cold, Timbers walked carefully to the middle of the road. She wanted to get back to the Goodladies junction where people could see and hear what was going on. Get near the people – that was the rule that all the girls had learned. Don't get caught in dark corners, or on waste ground near no houses, or in trees where everything remains hidden.

But the youths barred her way. At first, she counted three. One carried a cricket bat. Another juggled an iron bolt, the size of a cereal bowl, between his two hands.

"Run," said the little one on the left. He hardly looked old enough to be in long trousers.

"Yeah, run," taunted the subaltern. "You'd get nowhere in those high heels. We'd catch you in a hundred yards." Timbers was about to speak when the young bully giggled like a gangster. "Tee-hee. Hee-run. Yeah run." As he cackled, more youths appeared from the dark-

ness, in two's and three's until fifteen or twenty dirty faced schoolboys and hoodlums stood in the road. They came forward in an arc so
that soon not only was Timbers' route to the junction blocked but
also the pavements on either side of her. Still, the crowd hesitated to
get closer than ten yards.

Those boys who had been unarmed were picking up stones from
the gutter, or slipping belts from their trousers so that they could use
them as whips or their buckles as knuckle-dusters. She could have
kicked and slapped any one of them, and held their arms to their sides,
but Timbers was facing a mob.

Then the youths stopped moving about. Each stood quietly. Each
knew that the girl wasn't going to get away, but they feared what
would follow. They wanted someone else to start it.

"She's not a Frenchie!" one shouted.

"She dirties the streets just like one," argued the subaltern. "You've
heard her walking up and down at night, haven't you? Bothering, so
that you can't get to sleep for thinking of her. What's your mum and
dad said about her sort?"

"Ah, come on," drawled an impatient innocent from the back. "Are
we doing anything here or are we going on to the shops on London
Road?"

The first stone ricocheted two inches from Timbers' high heels.
The second caught her calf. She squealed.

"For God's sake run, you silly!" the subaltern shouted at her.

The mob moved forward. Timbers turned and bolted for the shelter of the church hall porch. Her screams excited her pursuers, who
were yelling and whistling as they caught up with her. She crouched
on the wet concrete floor, trying to get much of herself beneath the
stone bench.

A great cry went up, like a tribal hallowing.

Half a dozen were stoning her now.

"Harlot!"

The stones rebounded off the walls and ground. She counted the
first ones, flinching as they thudded into her back and ribs, but soon
so many were landing around her, glancing off her legs and hips, that
she lost herself in the nightmare. She dug herself further beneath the
bench – only an inch more protection but, when you know that you

79

cannot survive, every bit of cover seems like extra seconds of life. She wrapped her hands over the back of her head and pressed her face harder against the ground. Now, stones like rocks, like pebbles, like slithers of concrete were being thrown into her shelter. It felt as if people could not be delivering the force, as if it had to be nature spewing up anger from the earth or God delivering his punishment. Only one hit her face (and that was the only time that she gave way to tears, for she felt they would hit her face again and again) but so many bounced off her back and her hands covering her head that the pains became a pummelling.

She cried, and the stuff from her nose ran into her mouth, so that when she swallowed it tasted sour in her throat. She heard them coming. She couldn't see but she knew that the pack had to be at the very entrance of the porch because the stones were landing so hard and the smaller, sharper chips were ripping her skin like bullets.

They shouted 'Harlot!' again and again, like first formers when they have found a new word. Then the nastiest called a halt while he ran into the porch and stood behind her and shot his special stones, the ones he had been saving, at her buttocks and the bare thighs exposed by her crouching.

He kept it up for long minutes, his posse transfixed by the bravery of his outrage.

Then, suddenly, he had run out of ammunition and he stopped to breathe and look and wonder at what he had done. The shock of the cold picture – blood on her legs, her blouse torn, her arms and elbows scratched as if by barbed wire, and the grown woman, as old as their mothers, crying – scared many of his friends away. The five that stayed didn't know what to do next. "Bloody hell, Craig, we're not a lynching, are we? That's not the idea, is it?" The excitement, not the effort, had exhausted them and Thin Wayne's questions got them thinking as the hard core stood sticky and panting. Then they realised that they had been left behind; that they were no longer leaders and they might be missing something important. They ran off.

Timbers went on praying aloud, until she realised that they weren't coming back, then the praying turned to swearing as she carefully extricated herself from her hide. She scratched and fiddled, dabbed at herself for signs of blood. "You've stood on street corners in a worse state than this," she mumbled. "Get going. For God's sake girl, don't wait here. Get on with it. Get on with what you are." She needed to get her face right. She sucked through her nose. She rubbed her eyes and pinched her cheeks into place, like an old woman desperate to do what make-up couldn't. She worried over her stockings and shoes, and sorted out her breasts in her blouse. Then she made sure that her short skirt was covering just enough. "Stood on street corners in a worse state," she said again.

Stuart Morrison came forward from the night. A young boy, a little boy with his collar skew-whiff and his socks around his ankles. He was worried. His freckled cheeks were flat and his blinked uncertainly. He didn't understand what he had seen. He knew that he should have gone for his Dad, but it all happened so quickly. Now, he didn't know if he should approach the girl. "Are you all right Miss Timbers?" he asked. "I can take you home. M'mum'll give you some tea. She always does when I take people in." When Timbers didn't answer, he said, "Then let's sit together in the porch. For a few minutes, until you feel better."

"What do you know about it?" Timbers snapped.

He shook his head. Nothing. He knew nothing. He wasn't saying that he knew anything. He was just saying, that's all.

"Go on. Get off."

"Yes, Miss," he said.

Timbers muttered to herself. 'Bloody-stone-the-harlot!' Who had taught the urchins that sort of chant? Give them a few years and they'd come back, shy and fretful and wanting her to show them things down alleyways. She'd remember them. She'd remember each of their twenty faces and she'd charge them four times the rate and cheat them to boot. Timbers would get her own back.

She looked around for the lad but he had gone.

Jumpy and skittish, she found her way to the little bit of pavement on the corner of Goodladies Junction. Blame the mothers, she said. Hate the men, but blame the mothers. God – she sucked through her nose again – get it out of your head.

She tried to bring some order to the night. She looked around and listened and leant against brick walls that didn't move. Steely grey clouds turned almost blue when they passed over the rooftops; they looked like smoke over the city. The drizzle glistened in the mustard glow of the streetlamps. Like poisonous rain in a macabre film.

Timbers heard Slowly's sobs reaching out from the Hoboken's back garages. She was drunk again. Timbers pictured her sprawled in the gutter, her legs and raincoat muddy with rainwater. A woman from the houses shouted, "Shut up, you dirty old tramp." Another laughed rudely, a quarter of a mile off.

Twenty years on the streets had taught Timbers to battle hard, but 1964 had pushed her on the ropes so many times that she was beginning to ask what was she was fighting for. Other people were having fun – pop music, tele, open-topped cars, new clothes every week and sunny weather – but Timbers remembered standing in the rain on too many nights. She thought about the young girls who had worked on the pavements of Goodladies Road and moved on. Not always to better things but usually to a cleaner life. A life they could talk about. Then she thought about the old 'uns – Slowly, black Layna and herself – still doing it in the same place and with same men. (The faces changed but the men were same.)

A car slowed and a pug-chop face peered across from the driver's seat but, as soon as Timbers stepped forward, he pulled away. Timbers didn't give the rejection a second thought. It was still early. Then a pedestrian in an old-fashioned trilby and gabardine coat approached from Cardrew Street but when he was still twenty yards away, he crossed the road, whistling dolefully, so that he could safely pass on the opposite pavement. (Slowly would have shouted at him, if Slowly hadn't been incapable behind the garages.)

A wizened man with a grey face and woollen mittens came up to her. (This was Berkeley who hadn't worked for fourteen years and said that he hated women.) He asked if she was cold and if she had any sugar. He was short of sugar, he said, and the newsagent had closed at eight. Then he offered her fifty shillings.

"It's a fiver," Timbers said. "More if you want to do it indoors."

"Your place?"

"The garages. I've got one behind the Hoboken."

"Two pounds, ten. Come on girl, you've taken a beating, so you're damaged goods, aren't you? And what business are you going to do in the next five minutes? Bugger all, you know that. No-one's about.

There's nothing else for you, Timbs, and you could have fifty bob down your bra for hardly leaning backwards."

But Timbers wouldn't compromise.

"Well, I'm going into the Hoboken for a couple of brown ales. We'll see how you feel after that. Bloody cold, you'll be. And it'll be two quid then, you old brass."

At eleven thirty, chilled and lonely and doing no business, Timbers sneaked through the pub's back door and its square stone flagged kitchen, wanting the fag machine at the bottom of the staircase. Then she spotted young Baz Shipley, keeping out of Chloed's way. The girl wore a red leather mini skirt that Timbers hadn't seen before and she was sitting in a way that made Timbers look at her deep golden thighs.

"I've a man coming," she said.

Baz's mother pinched a bottle from beneath the bar and, within minutes, the two girls were drinking in the cubbyhole, sharing their grumbles beneath a bare light bulb. The gin and its glasses were set on a rickety table that looked as if it had come from a poor boy's wood-work class.

"Ma's promised him, so I'll have to wait."

"I've been chased up the street."

"He's right ugly," said Baz, pouring more drink. "I'll need this."

"Bloody schoolchildren. Twenty or thirty of them, there must have been."

"As long as he doesn't want to kiss me, I'll be all right." She swallowed the gin in one go. "I'll get him to do me while he's sitting down. That'll be all right. Have you ever had one die on you, Timbs? You must have done, sometime."

Timberdick shook her head. "Legs like yours. You should keep him looking and waiting until it's all over. Inspector Jen says you've got nice legs," she said.

"I know."

Timbers could hardly support her head. She leant forward and asked, "How." She mouthed the word again, as if she wanted to be sure the bones were still working. "How...do you know?"

"Bella told me. Jennifer said it when they were hiding in the cupboard and Bella told me. I think it's funny." And she laughed down her nose. "Do you know what I'm getting for Christmas, Timbs?

A topless dress. I've given Ma pictures of Garry Topes models and she's going to copy one."

Timbers thought, the fad will be over before Christmas. She had heard of girls being arrested in Brighton and Torquay but the Goodladies experience of the fashion craze was less newsworthy. Late in the summer, someone (probably Baz, although she never admitted it) put the word around that a lady in a topless dress would be appearing at the Hoboken on a darts night. The place was packed, and when the expectant spectators grew restless (and Ma Shipley was away at the loo) Baz slipped off her blouse and bra and paraded up and down the public bar. The reception was uproarious, but mother and daughter were banned for four weeks, a humiliation that Ma had not suffered in 56 years of drinking and was unlikely to forgive.

"You think your Ma's going to make you a topless dress after that night in here!"

"Do you know what I'd really like? A living room of my own. All my life I've had to share. With Ma, with you for a while and even when they locked me up for stealing, they put someone in with me. I'd just love to flop in front of the tele and know that no-one's going to walk in on me. I envy you, Timbs."

They said good-bye past twelve o'clock. The night was black now, with no moon, and the thundery clouds lay across the city, keeping the darkness in. It won't rain. There'll be no gale. It was a night when the air stews and takes your breath, like bad tobacco smoke in a kitchen. The dust and grit has got nowhere to go; it sticks in your throat and eyes. There had been a power cut in parts of the city, sending people to bed with socks or stockings on their feet and bicycle lamps to hand. As Timbers walked further from the Hoboken, even the streetlamps were out. Slates and windows rattled on the houses, because of the ghosts – there was no wind. The same ghosts that sounded like owls in the hidden alleys.

Timbers trod carefully. She was unsteady because of the drink and the pavements were broken and concrete steps stuck out from every doorway. She wasn't thinking about where she was going. She wanted to get home without doing any trade, so she kept to the back streets. She cut through a jitty and along the backs of houses and then she was lost. Not hopelessly lost – she had lived in these streets for too many years – but sufficiently confused to not know where she was. Timberdick didn't like drink. It made her talk in her head and knock into things, so she ended up with chips and grazes where her body had corners. Painfully thin, people said. The buggers, what did they know? Timbers was 34 yet had scabs on her knees and elbows like a truant tomboy. That's what painfully thin meant. Bloody scabs. Timbers leant against a lamp post and held her breath to stop herself retching. Recently Timberdick had spent a lot of time looking at herself. Her limbs were as stick-like as ever. She used to make jokes about sparrows legs and coat-hanger shoulders but now she worried about the state of her elbows and knees. Even when she was thinking about others things she would nervously pick at the wrinkles of tough skin. Time and again, she had stood in front of a mirror and studied her knees. It wasn't just that they were knocked and uneven; nowadays each joint seemed to rest uneasily in its socket. She wondered if a doctor would say there was something wrong. But her breasts were still good. There were not as perfect as they used to be but they were still large and proud. She had always said that her breasts could look after themselves and recently she had decided that she had good hips – small, square and compact – and her boy's bottom was as firm as it had ever been. She checked every morning but could detect no sign of her buttocks sagging. Ah, her face; of course, it was a funny one.

All this introspection was a response to something awful that had happened two weeks before. The episode was so absolutely awful that she had mentioned it to no-one. She had been with the young man twice before and as they thrashed about in the Hoboken's backyard, she thought that she was giving him what he wanted. He worked her arms and legs like levers and, you know, she had just the body for it. But as he was disengaging he looked at her private parts and, in an instant, turned his head and threw up. Men had been sick on her before – show her a working girl that hasn't suffered it – but Timbers had been looking at the expression on his face and she knew that it was the picture of her sex that had brought his stomach to his mouth. She went home and washed and shaved and, every day since, she rubbed in cream before she went to work so that she would smell sweetly. She thought about adding some cosmetic colour to her treasures. She cried at night as she realised that she was turning into an old bag.

As she turned into her street, she kept her eyes down to the pavement. Her head lolled to one side like a doll's with a broken neck. She saw a housewife on the other side of the road. She wore an overcoat, red and black check, and a scarf that didn't match.

Glenys Seaton had been waiting for two hours, wondering what sort of lady lived behind the brown painted door. She was a woman who couldn't paint, that was certain. She had laid on the colour with a ladle and made no attempt to smooth out the runs. Her nets were freshly dipped, yes. And the doorstep was scuffed but not muddy. (No-one did doorsteps like they used to do. Women didn't like to clean in public anymore. It was all right for a man to wash his car at the roadside, but did you ever see a woman bulling-up the threshold to her home?)

She crossed as Timbers reached her front door. She came carrying bags and a Hessian sack, her coat open to the cold night and one foot at odds with the other.

"May I speak with you?"

Timbers was trying to get the Yale key in its lock. "Have you ever been skinny?"

"No."

"Do you knock into things?"

No. Her limp had taught her to be careful.

"Then you don't know enough to talk about anything."

"Please, I need your help."

Timbers thought that she wanted a hand with her bags but the women made no move to give them up.

"They're some 78's from my husband," she said, lifting the sack. "The most valuable thing we have, he always said."

"Not more bloody records. Jazz are they? Why would I want them?"

"Perhaps you don't, but I have so little to offer you."

Timbers was ready tell her to bugger off.

"My name is Mrs Jones."

"Bloody rare, that."

"Glenys Jones."

"A Welsh Jones. Even rarer."

"No, I'm not Welsh. I come from Aylesbury." Timber saw that the woman was blushing. Mrs Jones rubbed her fingers across her eyes. "God, I don't know why I'm telling you this. My mother didn't know Glenys was a Welsh name. The thing is, my daughter tried to shoot you."

Timbers had the door open. She held its edge to steady her as she turned to look the woman in the face. "She tried to kill me. That's what she did."

Mrs Jones bit her lip to keep the tears at bay. "Lord above, she's sixteen, barely out of school. Her dad's been murdered."

Timbers didn't say anything but let the woman follow her into the house.

"You're name isn't Mrs Jones, not if you were married to Donald Seaton."

"I know, I...didn't think. I was walking across the road to meet you and I wanted to introduce myself as Glenys Jones. That's who I was to start off with. What with Donald being dead and the children growing away from me. I'm sorry, it was a silly thing to say, 'Mrs Jones'. It didn't mean anything. Look, Cynthia made a mistake."

"You're telling me!"

"She thought you were my husband's lover. She knew that he was meeting his woman at the railway station and she wanted to spy on them. Can't you see? Cynth saw you by the railway carriages and thought you'd killed her father. Lord above, she's only a teenager. Who knows how her mind works?"

"I never met your husband. As far as I know."

"Well," said Mrs Seaton. "You and I will never know for sure, will we?"

Leaving the front door open so that the strange woman could trail after her, Timbers walked unsteadily to her living room. She winced when Mrs Seaton switched on a light and said no when she offered to make tea. "Let me get m'fags out," said Timbers.

"No. You sit down, my dear. You've cut your face, I can see that now. And there's blood on the back of your leg."

"I've been bloody stoned, like a harlot in the Bible. Fifty to a hundred of them, hurling bricks and iron bars at me and shouting abuse that they could only have learned from their mothers. No man'd ever swear like that." She felt the drink churn in her stomach and she held it still with a hand. "Two hundred of them in the street, stoning me."

Mrs Seaton got down on her knees, fussed through her very large handbag and produced a handkerchief damp with iodine that she laid against Timbers grazed cheek. "Now, we're not friends, so you just call me 'Mrs S.' That's friendly, but not friends." When Timbers didn't argue, she pressed further, "We need to rebuild you, don't we. I'll start with the house; it needs tidying. Then I'll visit you again and we'll talk. And we'll talk about the way you dress."

"A right bloody sister of mercy, aren't we?" But Timbers couldn't say more; she needed to hold her breath in.

"Miss Timberdick, if I may say so, you are too drunk to argue with me. Now, slip down to the carpet, in case you are sick – it's easier to clean a carpet than an armchair – and look at me while I make a start."

She went to the kitchen and returned with hot Oxo in a mug. "I've looked in your pantry, dear. Is that what you call the cupboard where the kettle stands? Well, you really ought to belong to a Christmas club at this time of year. Fine Fare do a very reasonable one. You get an extra thr'pence for every five shillings you save."

Timbers laughed. She couldn't believe that this woman was advising her to open an account with a grocer. I mean, girls like Timbers don't.

"And powdered coffee's another thing. It's simply rubbish, dear. A waste. You wouldn't entertain powdered eggs. We all remember what they tasted like in the war. The little bits of sand stuck to your teeth. No, you'll find Camp Coffee far more satisfying. Yes, at two and seven pence halfpenny, it's more expensive, cup for cup. But you'll need to drink fewer cups because it's more satisfying."

Mrs S hoovered, she dusted, she wiped and she polished. In half an hour, Timbers was laughing as if she had never laughed before. Red-faced laughter, so convulsive that she had to snort through her nose to get air into her lungs. She was sitting on the floor with her arms holding her knees close to her chest and when Mrs Seaton said, 'Grubby grouting, Little Timbers,' Little Timbers' toes came off the carpet and she rocked on the bones of her bottom. The woman took a hatpin from inside the hem of her dress, crouched on the carpet and put her face down to the hearth; then she started to needle the dirt from the cement between the tiles. "One of the tests of thorough housewifery," she said, though Timbers was laughing too much to hear properly. She fell on her sides, her hands clutching her stomach.

Now, Timberdick had become the spectacle. Mrs Seaton sat on the rug and waited for the girl's antics to settle down. "I know you have to humiliate me. I know that's part of your making the most of it. Me, needing to beg you. You, making me know that I have nothing you need. Well, I can clean for you. It's what I do. I 'do' for other people. Since I was a young girl and ever since I've been married. I will stay all night, if you like, and clean your home, if you'll let Cynthia off. I have to pay, I know that. My daughter tried to kill you but my husband is dead, so who else will protect her. Shield her from her foolishness. It has to be me. I have to give you whatever I can."

Timbers gave no permission and certainly no welcome. She left Mrs Seaton at work on the hearth and went quietly to the kitchen, where she washed without taking off any clothes before withdrawing to her bedroom. She left the light off, undressed to her knickers, then laid herself in her bed, folding the sheets and blankets around her little body. As she settled, the nausea from the night's drinking, which had been kept at bay by her laughing, came back to her. Her stomach felt cold and, when holding it in her hands failed to warm it, she pulled a pillow from beneath her head and pressed it against her middle. The sounds of her new housemaid, cleaning and clearing up in the next room, settled her down and she fell asleep with those sounds in her head (and no fear of nightmares). But she could not have slept for long because when she opened her eyes, her cheeks still flat on the mattress, Mrs Seaton was placing a beaker of hot milk on the bedside table.

"Don't disturb yourself, child."

The room was still dark, although a bare bulb in the kitchen was sufficient to give the bedroom some shapes and shadows. Mrs Seaton took the chair from the dressing table and placed it in the corner, not far from Timbers' head. She began, "I've known about Donald's girlfriends for years. I think he started his first affair within a year of our wedding. We even found that we could talk about his wanderings-off. In general terms, you understand. And when we were older, of course, when things don't matter so much. That's what he said. He said, it was all a tribute to me. The first time we made love, I was so perfect for him that he longed to feel that magic again. Since I was no longer new to him, this was difficult, of course. He said 'of course'. I didn't. That's why he began to search elsewhere. He said it was like liking good jazz."

Timbers whispered, "Liking good jazz?"

"It was Donald's little saying. He said that the first time you hear good jazz, it's so exciting that you carry on searching for the same thrill. Again and again. And he was looking for another girl who could make him feel as I had done, that first time. It was a tribute to me. He was always saying it was a tribute."

Timbers' smile owed nothing to Mrs Seaton's story. There was a very satisfied look on her face but there was no smugness in it. When she closed her eyes and listened to the older woman talking and when the woman repeatedly called her 'child', Timbers allowed herself to think that she was recovering the sensation she had been denied as a child; she was being told a bedtime story. This was the quality time the young Timbers should have known with her mother.

"You know that Barbara Bellamy was one of his old ones? They met when we were buying her house, but Donald didn't get his feet under her table until May this year. I think she was very pleased that he should two-time with her; of course, the vicious devil didn't know that he was cheating on her just as much as he was cheating on me. He'd been with his dear Susannah since November. You'd like her, my child, Miss Susannah Thompson. She's a very good lady."

She has good grouting, Timbers teased in her head.

"And she wouldn't put up with Donald's other women. Other than her, that is. 'Other', including me. Oh, she knows her place and every-one else's, does Miss Susannah. Donald broke things off with Barbara at the end of the summer and he tried to make things intolerable for me. By making his adultery clear. Phone calls, letters, even photo-graphs. He just left them around for me to find. The problem was Cynth." She sighed, "Cynth was the problem. She saw all these clues and felt cheated. She wanted to do something about it. She found out that he was coming home from London on the night of the crash and he planned to meet his lover at the end of the line. Cynth decided to confront them. Of course it didn't work out like that, but she saw you, Little Timbers, and thought you were his woman. She decided that you had spoiled her father's life and caused his death. He was on the train because of you, that's how she saw it. That's why she shot you. You won't tell your policeman, will you, Miss Timberdick? Promise me that." But 'Little Timbers' was already asleep and a night that had held such horrors, drifted away in something like fairy-tales and soft blankets.

* * *

Timbers was woken by cooking smells. She left her bed and leant against the doorframe between her room and the kitchenette. She was naked on purpose; she wanted to see the woman's reaction.

"I've been home," Mrs S remarked without turning around. She had heard her new mistress get up but hadn't seen her yet. "I wouldn't want you to think that I've been here all night. I borrowed a key from your hook, while you were asleep. I hope you don't mind. If I'm going to clean for you, I must get one of my own. I can do Tuesdays and Thursdays, and Fridays very occasionally." She placed the fried egg and bacon on a plate and turned to see Timbers. "Very nice, dear. Now put some clothes on so I won't have to tell you what I really think."

No-one had spoken to Timberdick Woodcock like that before. Or, if they had, Timbers hadn't tolerated it. Naughtily, Timbers tried again to shock the woman. "Have you ever fed anyone in the bath. I mean, there's never enough water in the mornings for a deep bath but it still could be fun."

"No, dear. Not fun. Just difficult. I don't see how you could conduct your table manners in a bath. We eat at a table, don't we? Never on our laps and certainly not in bed. Unless womanly matters persuade us."

"But you let Donald walk all over you," said Timbers, still at the bedroom door and still bare.

"I allowed his affairs, yes. Because of our child. But I never allowed further intimacy between us. Shall I collect the post? Don't worry about getting dressed, dear. I'd catch cold, if I was you; that'll show everyone who's in charge."

Timbers found her out of shape dressing gown and took her breakfast to the only table in the flat. In the corner of the living room, where no-one went.

Mrs S returned with one letter and a parcel. She gave the letter to Timbers but insisted that the girl should put down her knife and fork before she opened it. "And finish your mouthful before attempting to read. It avoids any temptation to talk while chewing. We are rebuilding you, remember?"

Timberdick read, 'I made the train crash with things on the line. Because I wanted making love in a train to be part of something big. Now I cannot live with it. I will be dead before you read this. You are the only person who knows everything. Does my wife deserve the shame of public knowledge? You must decide that.'

Claptrap, Timbers thought. These weren't the words of a suicidal man. Men on the edge had given her a seeing-to, many times; she knew what they sounded like.

"What is it?"

"A bloke that's all."

The letter went on, 'I saw the baby's mother. She was forty or fifty and wore a tartan cloak that made her look well-to-do. Your baby will be well cared for, so don't worry.'

Timbers looked up and saw Mrs S cutting the string from the parcel. "What are you doing?"

"Unwrapping it. You're busy with that one. It can't be just a bloke, because you're going on reading it."

"It's my bloody letter and that's my bloody parcel." She snatched the package. "Look, you're too much. The mornings are special to me. Half past eleven until two o'clock. I try not to work mornings, these days. And I like to laze on my own in my dressing gown, reading a lovey-dovey until the tele comes on at dinner. I don't want to be busy-bodied."

"I'm sorry."

"I've even joined the library."

Mrs S accepted the rebuke but said, "I'm sorry, Timberdick," without feeling. And she put no 'Miss' in front of the name, Timbers noticed.

Timbers threw the package back. "Oh, go on. It's knickers from old Leapers."

"His underpants!"

"No, Fruit-Cake, mine. He wanted to wash and iron them."

"Fruit-Cake?"

"Well, what can I call you? You're bonkers, for God's sake. A heart of gold, yes – and people must love you – but you're looney."

Again, Mrs S accepted the unkindness. She said, "Your underpants?"

"He wanted to wash and iron them."

"Did he?"

"Well, he had dirtied them in the first place, by squashing chocolate cake inside, then squeezing the goo and crumbs into everywhere."

"Good Gracious. How did you both manage it without making a mess on the sheets?"

"I was standing up, admiring an old jazz record. I looked a bit like a statue while he crawled around, getting on with it. Crumbling, squeezing, pushing and poking, sliding. Getting chocolate into everything in my knickers."

"Yes, dear. Well enough, I'm sure. Was he an odd fellow?"

"Show me a man who isn't these days," Timbers sighed. "It's the bomb."

"Ah yes, the bomb. The bomb?"

"Remember what you said about liking good jazz? Well, I was that moment for him."

"You won't let him have our records, will you?"

"No, I'm going to give them to a special friend. A policeman. He likes odd-ball stuff."

"Well, you tell him, they're very valuable. Only five copies made, Donald said, and it's Jimmy McPartland. They've got 'To Marian' written on the labels.[5]"

Timbers wouldn't talk about the records. Instead, she caught hold of the woman's wrists and made her sit on the carpet, next to her chair. "Where is she? You've not mentioned that she's missing, but

---

[5]Timbers never gave them to me but when the Hoboken burned down – two years later – I found them in the debris. There's no proof that Jimmy McPartland is the jazzman but, when I showed them to an experienced dealer in the eighties, she immediately identified them and offered a story to account for their manufacture – in Birmingham, England, she said. 'Marian' was McPartland's English wife.

that's why you're here."

Tears hid in her reply. "I wanted to plead for her."

"That's not why you've stayed."

"Your man on the lines," said Mrs Seaton, wanting to be free of Timbers grasp, so that she could rub the water in her eyes. "The Man from Scurries. He caught up with her after the shooting and took her away. God knows what will happen to her now."

Mrs S produced a single page of Basildon Bond from her handbag. "It's anonymous," she said as she passed it over. "The writing's clumsy and, look, the paper's crumpled where they've screwed it up. As if they decided not to send it but changed their mind."

The note warned Cynthia's mother that the girl was in danger. 'Scurries is the danger,' it said. 'I know what he can do.'

"When did you get this?"

"What do you mean?"

"Work it out. It must have been written before Cynthia tried to shoot me. How else could it have been delivered to you by now?"

"Look. No. I think. I'm not sure, I think it must have been delivered by hand."

"Where were you when your husband was murdered, Mrs Seaton?"

The woman relented. "All right. I was at the station. I was looking for Cynthia. I wanted to stop her from doing something stupid."

Timberdick sat still. She looked at the woman's face and said, "No."

"All right. I knew that Barbara Bellamy and Donald were going to be there and I wanted to face them."

"Why? The affair was over, you say."

"Not about the affair." Mrs Seaton wasted no time on being irritated by Timbers' question. She explained, "I found out that when Donald bought the house he also bought a little investment in her shop. Nothing wrong in that, of course, but he forgot to tell his wife. Now, what with Susannah's demands and everything, they were going to sell the shop together. That's what the trip to London was about."

"They travelled together?"

"Of course they travelled together. They were old lovers, weren't they? Well, I wanted some of the money. That's fair, isn't it? Look, what was fair about them selling it behind my back?"

Eight

A Second Chapter of Witnesses

Joe Lamey had been told to stay away from trains. He had nowhere to go but the railwayman's social club. When Timbers found him there at half past ten on Friday morning, he was sitting in the lounge bar, alone with the committee's accounts. He looked a sorry man. His sallow cheeks had been roughened by three days of not shaving and his long limbs showed the restlessness of a man used to standing up and getting on with things.

"They don't let you drive again until your boss has sat in the cab with you," he explained. "Mine says I'm still a worry. I don't think that's a-been said to anyone, ever. It were only a derailment, I told him. You want a drink, Miss?"

Before Timbers could reply, he had stood up from his chair, stretched, and hurried to the counter. He returned with an orange juice, and nothing for himself. "I'm worrying that you're interfering with my Lucy, Miss. If I'm honest, I has to say it. Your pal's been up to her little garage asking questions. Just because she were there, and that's not fair. Our Lucy's been ill, like. Do you know that? And your pal's been bothering her and the dead man's daughter and her friend – he's a ne'er do well, that one."

Timbers thought, he's got sour but honest eyes. She said, "Mr Lamey, you're the only one who can help me."

"We had to send her aways for months. Things was getting on top of her."

The club steward had arrived and was keeping an eye on them as he went about his business. (The lads didn't want people questioning the engine driver until the enquiry was over.)

"No-one will trouble your daughter, Mr Lamey. I promise."

"You know who did it then? Who a-murdered my passenger?"

Timbers shook her head. "You and Lucy were there. And Miss Bellamy. I was there with Scurries. Then, Cynthia Seaton and her mother. Six of us."

"And Leaper."

"Yes, he's number seven. I want you to explain the workings, Mr Lamey. Fred Leaper said that I had to free the hook-nut where carriages join. He said that would take the weight away from the back plate. He tried to explain it but I couldn't see how it was all connected. He said it would free the coaches so that they wouldn't fall over."

"A load of hog-wash," Joe Lamey said. "Leaper's had no a-commendation from the board, you know that? No expressions of worthiness from the Chief Constable or the Chief Fire Officer. Because they can see it for what it is. Buckets of hogwash. My train weren't going to fall from the road bridge. It a-barely left the tracks at all. And all this stuff he got you to do – just clearing away debris, that's all it were."

"But I heard the train moving."

"You heard metal falling on hardcore, girl. Debris. You shifts one bit of debris and disturbs twenty others. Doing it's dangerous, if you ask me. The question is; were Leaper fibbing or just in a panic?"

"So tell me."

"He's always been a-scared of crashes. It's been on his mind from the first day I knew him. What would he do? Would he panic? You know the sort of questions. So, when it happened, he a-makes up his own story of it, doesn't he? I reckon he believes it, you know, and that doesn't make him a liar. Look, Fred Leaper had to concentrate on one thing. That'd be his only way of a-dealing with a crash." Lamey shrugged his shoulders. "For some reason, he thought that the wreck were going to move and he let the notion fill his head completely."

"Will you tell me about the crash?"

"No."

"Please."

"I've already told the Railway Police and the Regional Manager. I weren't hurrying. Signals at Willersley Halt had made me late and I had no distance to make up the time in, so I weren't hurrying. We was at Willersley for ten minutes, I reckon. They'd have checked it all through with the guard. He left the train, you see, and went to the phone at the trackside. Then when we got going again, it were seven miles and we was just curving into the station when I felt something under my wheels. Iron bars, I reckon. Lengths of steel."

"Was it a tadpole?"

"A tadpole, my girl. Now what do you know about tadpoles?"

"Someone said it was, that's all."

"Well, it were. Front half thirteen inches wider than the second half."[6]

"So, if you were parked on a bend, at Willersley, you might not have seen someone leaving the second half of the train."

"I'd have a-seen them on the track, of course I would."

"...But not leaving the carriages."

"...But anyone who killed our Mr Seaton wouldn't be leaving by the back half of the train. He were in the front and there were no passage between the carriages. They'd have stayed on board until they got to the station."

"Not if they saw Willersley Halt as their opportunity. Perhaps they got off the train, wanting to board the first carriage, but you drove off before they had chance to get to Seaton"

"Then they'd a-be off the train and they'd have to beat me to the station."

"Did you see anything before the crash?"

"I've told the enquiry what I saw. That'll do."

"And Leaper found you on the ground."

"He found me on the bank and helped me to Lucy's car. Then Lucy and me was together for the rest of the night."

"And you didn't see anyone else?"

"I saw the Bellamy woman. She didn't see me because I were

---

[6]Eighteen months after the murder, the local Model Railway Society provoked a long debate by including a tadpole in their representation of the accident. Some enthusiasts produced evidence that a 'tad' could not have worked the line in 1964. Others found witnesses – and some handwritten journals from train spotters – who reported that tadpoles had been there. Leaper and Lamey would never talk about it. But in 1967 a teenager walked up and down Goodladies Road looking for the prostitute who could settle the argument. "She'd know by the hoses," he explained to any girl who'd listen.

slumped down. But I saw her." He hesitated, then admitted, "All right Lucy weren't with me all the time. When Bellamy walked past, Lucy were out of the car, looking for Leaper. But I could see and she didn't go near Seaton. We didn't even know where he were. Not then, we didn't."

"So when did you decide to drive the train, Mr Lamey? Fred Leaper didn't know you were due."

"So do I have to check with a porter before I can swap a trip? The train were taking me home, weren't it? Weren't it natural for me to say I'd take it and not the rostered driver? It happens all the time, Miss. I'll tell you, Miss, they know something's wrong with things. Me, I'm still on a-sick leave as the world knows I shouldn't be. And Fred Leapers a-been suspended because they found the 'Ladies Waiting' unlocked and a bed made up. Hogwash. They know the thing was done on purpose and they won't let either of us back until it's sorted."

Timbers thought about laying a hand on his lap, but she didn't.

"We're suspended," he said and it shamed him.

* * *

Out on the streets, Timbers leaned on the tubular railing and watched the traffic bunch at the lights. The city's full of old motors, she thought, patched with bits of old Macintoshes and held together with leather straps and string. The drivers thought they would be good for another two thousand miles. Short journeys to work each day and run outs at weekends. Surely, it was nonsense. Didn't people in this city buy as many new cars as folk in other cities? But, once the idea was in Timbers' head and she began to search for any vehicle with 1964's number plate, the fib got stubborn; it refused to be proved wrong. My God, we're poor, she thought. All of us. Here, crowds of people went about on bicycles, sometimes four or five abreast so that the buses couldn't get through. When the buses caught up with each other, they progressed along the road in convoys of three or more.

She hadn't come here to count the buses. (That was her boredom.) She had walked the fifty yards from the Railway Club so that she could discover affairs at Scurries, the suit shop. Scurries hadn't the standing of Dunns or Gieves and Hawkes but it had secured a dependable clientele of office managers, bachelor uncles, headmasters from county schools and army officers on pensions. The firm owned three branches; this was their largest employing a newly appointed manager, an experienced salesman (Timbers' Man from Scurries) and a lad of eighteen. But the Man from Scurries wasn't in today. Timbers had phoned from the kiosk on the corner and had been told - rather curtly because there was no good reason for a common sounding woman to be phoning for him – that he hadn't been seen since Monday and was unlikely to be in before early closing on Wednesday.

Timbers' legs were cold and damp. She shifted them as she lent her crossed arms on the railing. She wasn't wearing a coat but the long sleeve cardigan that she had worn on her night on the railway tracks. It was long enough to cover her mini skirt so that, if anyone looked at her from behind, they might fancy that she was wearing nothing underneath. (Timbers liked to wear things that way. Really childish, she sometimes thought.)

A quiet and polite voice said, "I'm looking for some company."

He was in his forties with a cropped haircut, a round face – slightly too red – and he wore a pressed sports jacket over a check shirt with a knitted tie. Brown brogues, Timbers guessed without looking. She said, "I'm not working. Bugger off."

She went on looking at the shop across the street. A bus ploughed through the wet gutter causing her to step back. The tidy gentleman put out a hand to stop her tripping over herself.

"Look, bugger off. I'm looking for someone." Then, relenting slightly, "Look, catch me round the Hoboken tonight."

"No. That really won't do."

He spoke precisely and softly. Like a doctor, Timbers thought. Probably, he was one.

"I know your name's Timberdick."

"Yes, you probably dream about me at night."

The door to the outfitters opened and Jennie Hillier walked out. She paused to look up at the uncertain sky, then buttoned her raincoat across her chest and marched towards the busy traffic lights. Timbers meant to intercept her at the crossing but her neatly dressed prospect stood in her way. "Really, it will cause trouble if you don't spare me a few minutes," he said.

Timbers sighed petulantly. "What do you want?"

"Twenty minutes, no more. And I do have a room."

"Eight quid ten," she said, hoping that twice her going rate would put him off. When he produced his wallet, Timbers was sure she'd been set up.

She looked around for a plain clothed policeman, ready to arrest her. Then she looked her man starkly in the face. "Copper!"

"No, no. Please." He was dithering now.

"Then let's get away from here. You daft bugger, paying me out on the bloody street."

They were Hoovering the stairs at the Aintree Arms. When Timbers picked her way through the leads and hoses, the cleaners looked up to see if the gentleman was embarrassed. The two ladies couldn't speak above the noise of the vacuums but they exchanged nods and glances. They had got his room number. Later, they would recite the details over cups of tea.

The man in the knitted tie unlocked Number 42 and held the door as Timbers pushed past him.

Scurries was sitting up in the bed. He wore striped Viyella pyjamas and his hair had been parted with a wet comb. The blankets came up to his chest and his top button was done up. Timbers remembered how he had looked in the train. An apprentice boy at Blackpool. Now he was a sick boy in bed. She thought, Betty 'Slowly' Barnes would suit you, you chubby mouse. She's used to treating men like naughty boys. She'd make a good school matron. She'd spoon foul medicine down your throat and pinch your nose until you swallowed.

"Bloody nerve!" Timbers shouted.

"No, no," said her doctor-type. "You mustn't misunderstand. He wants to explain things to you, that's all." He moved to a chair by the window.

Timbers stood still and accused, "You caught up with the girl after the shooting."

Scurries nodded.

She said, "Her name's Cynthia Seaton, the dead bloke's daughter. I know her mother and I want to know what you're doing with her."

He shook his head. He kept his mouth closed and his jaws sucked in. Timbers wondered if he had a cough lozenge under his tongue. "Nothing," he mumbled. "Really, nothing like that. I just wanted to ask her what she saw during the night. Miss Timberdick, they're going to sack me. I've...I've been told to leave home and my wife won't let me see the children. I need to know that you're not going to tell anyone about the train crash."

"So, you caused it?"

"When Beryl Shipley – Baz, you call her – told me that you would definitely spend the night with me and I was to meet you at the top of Old Moore's Lane, well, it was too soon, of course. I had to drive over to the sidings and lay the obstructions across the main line. I had to make sure that I didn't get dirty and still get back to Moore's Lane for you. That's why I was late."

"But why'd you do it?"

"Because I wanted to hear a train crashing while we were making love. It has always been part of my dream."

So what makes you think that we were making love? It was uncooked sex in a cold place. And don't fret about losing out; I'd have mucked it up for you. She asked, "Did you know Donald Seaton was on board?"

"No. Nor Mrs Bellamy from my dress shop."

"Who did you see on the lines?"

"The woman with the baby, Timbers. She collected it after you left. She was forty-ish, very smartly dressed. She carried the cot along the main platform and I saw her get into a car."

The man in the corner tried to say that Timbers had asked enough questions, but she cut him off. "Why'd you run off?"

"I couldn't afford for people to find out what I'd been doing with you. You can understand that."

"And why'd you come to see me outside the Hoboken?"

"I wasn't looking for you. I'd followed the girl to the pub and I was waiting for her to come out. I wanted to ask her what she'd seen on the lines. God, I didn't know she was going to shoot you."

"Where is she now?"

"I don't know. God, am I supposed to be looking after her?"

"You bloody know!"

The Doctor got to his feet. "Now..."

"It's all right. I'm not going to hit him. Just tell me why you wrote the letter."

"I wanted to disappear. I thought that I would pretend to be dead. But now, Leonard has explained that I can start my life anew without that."

"From the church is he?"

Leonard insisted that he wasn't from the church. He had wanted to be a doctor once, he said, if it was any of Timbers' business. He had a great many medical books at home.

She asked for her eight pounds and ten shillings. Not because she had done anything in the bedroom but because they had tricked her into coming. She settled for three pound notes, and was folding them into her bra as she walked down the staircase.

What did he mean? His dress shop?

The ladies on the stairs said that he couldn't have been up to much; she'd been less than ten minutes.

'Lean' Boots and Matt Hughes were drinking with the barman in the public. Timbers got between them and asked for a gin and lime. She noticed that neither of the boys patted her bottom or tried to lean against the shape of her breasts. Two years ago, she would have had to tell them off for that.

"I've got a job for you," she said.

The barman interrupted smartly. "Then you'd better discuss it away from here. Go over to the corner." He looked at the pub's clock. "This place will be heaving in twenty minutes, so get your business sorted and get out. The governor's trying to clean the place up." He gave them drinks on the house.

"What's it worth?" Boots asked as they organised themselves at the little round table.

"Not you, that's for sure," said Hughes.

The boys had grown up together and delivered their repartee – one line to one, the next to the other – like a double act on stage. Yes, there was something comic about them. They were little and quick witted, always ready with a jibe.

"Is that right? Your old copper's ditched you?"

"He's never had me," Timbers countered.

"Oh, not many!" laughed Master Hughes. "Old Timberdick! Been on the streets since before the streets were invented."

It hurt. She couldn't pretend that it didn't.

"He's with another tart now," teased Boots.

Timber said, "Bullshit. No-one'd have him. Fat old bugger. It's just a story he's putting about. He wants the young 'uns to think he's still got it in him."

They leaned forward together. "Do you want us to describe her?" Timbers waited.

"Now, be patient," roared Hughes. "It'll come to me 'slowly'."

They laughed, but Timbers didn't understand. She said, "I've got a job for you."

"What's it about?" Boots was serious now.

"You're good boys and I don't want you to get into trouble, so you'll have to be good at it."

"You want us to steal a motor?"

"I want you to borrow one, just for a couple of hours. I want you to see how fast it can go. Take it up to Willersley Halt and then race it back to the city. You put it back where you found it, understand? The owner's a nice girl."

"A nice girl," drooled Hughes. "Hey. You've not told us what's in it for us."

"What d'you want?"

"Black Layna," they said together. "It's got to be her. Bootsie straight away, then me after the job's done."

"I'll speak to her," said Timbers. "I can't promise anything."

When the boys got to their feet, Hughes bent forward so that his stale smelling mouth was close to Timbers' face. "You'd better promise. Because me and Boots'll get you nicked otherwise."

They went off laughing.

The Aintree was filling up with part time workmen who had finished their shifts and tradesmen who worked out of sight of their bosses. Timbers had been sitting alone for only a few minutes, when the barman approached her table. "The governor won't have it, duck. A woman on her own in the public."

"Do us a good turn, Harry. Give Shooter's Grove a ring and ask Jennifer Hiller to come down."

"You in trouble, Tee?"

103

"As soon as I get up in the morning, yeah? Always the same, isn't it?"

He collected the empties, polished the tabletop and walked off. Hardly a minute had passed when a man with a wire-haired terrier arrived with two drinks. "Harry says," he said and sat down. They didn't speak. He fussed with the dog and Timbers pretended to look through the frosted glass windows. A couple of his mates pulled his leg, but there was no harm in the jokes.

Timberdick spent an easy twenty minutes, looking at the characters – ignoring those who tried to catch her eye – listening to the sounds on the pavements outside and keeping her legs tucked under the table. She finished her drink and told the little man to get her another.

"Harry says I'm not to leave you alone."

"Well, we can't bloody both go up. And I'm dying of thirst, here."

"You can look after Wellington, then."

"Bloody can't. Take him with you."

Jennifer Hillier arrived when he was away from the table. Lord, she looked out of place. She had changed into civilian clothes. Furry boots and doubled over coat cuffs. As if she was going to stand in the cold on Bonfire Night. She stood at Timberdick's table and waited to be told something.

"Do you want to take your coat off or put your collar down?"

"I don't want to be seen."

"Don't be daft. Everyone's had a bloody good look at you. Dressed up like a pantomime cow. God, your mother's got a lot to answer for."

Jennie sat down and took two cigarettes from her handbag. "Why do you want to see me?"

"Because you used to be a detective," said Timbers.

The little man returned with three drinks on a tray and the dog tied to his arm. Jennie helped him land the glasses on the table and asked if he would be joining them.

"No, he won't. Bugger off, John."

Neither of the women looked at him again. Jennie leaned forward and said, "Timbers, I've something to tell you."

"So have I. I know who crashed the train. I can't give you his name."

"Scurries?"

"That's right."

Jennifer understood. "He's not been into his shop since, but they received a suicide note from him this morning. He's not dead; they've seen him at the windows of this place, upstairs."

"What are you going to do?"

"Timbers, I need to get back into CID. This might just be my opportunity but I've got to time it right. The Railway Police are in the way at the moment, so I'll give Scurries a few more days."

Timbers added to the story. "He says he saw Cynthia Seaton at the scene of the crash. She was spying on her father. That's why she tried to shoot me. Because she saw me and thought that I was his lover. And he says he saw the mother collect my baby. I can't tell you her name."

"Susannah Thompson?"

"That's right."

"An ambulance driver saw her car at the station. He told me about it while you were locked in the toilets. I've traced the number."

"Jen, don't tell. I'm going to call on her this afternoon. I want to be sure we do things right for the little baby."

"What do you think I'm going to do? I mean, who'd I tell? A mother took her baby out at night. That's hardly neglect, Timbers. She can't have left the little one alone for more than a few moments. Hardly abandonment, is it?" She asked, "Do you know who killed Seaton?"

"I don't care. I need to make sure that the baby's all right and I want to be sure that Scurries doesn't get his fingernails into Cynthia Seaton."

"They call her Cynful, you know," Jennifer said. "Someone told me. I can't tell you their name."

"Say, you've got to meet her mother. She's a scream!"

"Timbers, I've something to tell you."

"About Ned, is it? Two lads in here said he's seeing someone else. I don't care. I mean, why should I?"

"He'd tell you, Timbs. He'd tell us both. No, don't listen to gossip. Ned Machray's old and fat and I think he smells with his shoes off. No one would be interested in him. No, now listen, I have something to tell you."

105

"Yeah, you have!" Timbers joined in. She was enjoying a conversation with this Police Inspector for the first time. "You disappeared into a cupboard with Bella. She had her breasts out and everything. So, come on. Have you seen her again?"

"No." The mother's daughter turned crimson. "No, but I do have another friend, Timbers, who is just out of this world. Of course," she said, taking up her drink. "I can't give you a name."

* * *

In a week of damp and drizzle, the sun broke out on Friday afternoon and, for five hours, the city had space for good news. Timberdick caught a bus to Lightinghouse. Lightinghouse had been a factory where women in hats poured soup crystals into little boxes that leaked onto the floor. Now, it was an urban village for folk who had retired well off. Timberdick walked for fifteen minutes, resting now and then on benches on the grass verges or leaning against the trees that said this was a good part of town. She settled, like a songbird settles when it has nowhere to go, on a low brick garden wall. The lady from Number Sixty didn't mind, because she was out. Number Sixty Three was across the road. She sat and a couple of men past fifty looked at her. She wondered what it was like to live in these houses, knowing that you had done well and got your reward. She hadn't intended to call on Number Sixty Three but the curtains twitched more than two or three times. The young woman inside was interested in her, so Timberdick got off the wall, walked across the street and knocked on the door. Because there was no answer, and because Timbers didn't want people staring at her from nearby houses, she opened a side gate and stepped into the back garden.

Next door, an eight year old was cleaning his bike against the side wall of the house. He had a bowl of soapy water, a bowl of clean water for rinsing and a bowl of dirty water. While he worked with a toothbrush on the fiddly bits, he recited a perfect verse of She Loves You (already an old hit). He had folded a coarse floorcloth and a clean chamois over the cycle crossbar. His cowboy hat, holster and six-shooter hung from the fence between the two properties. He regarded Timberdick with curiosity rather than suspicion. He knew that he was intelligent – people had written that down for others to read – so he needed to show Timbers that he was a step ahead of her.

"You're Mrs Thompson's sister," he said. "I can let you in. I've already let your daughter through the French windows. Mrs Thompson's taken Jamie for a walk. She won't be back for twenty minutes, but I can make you a pot of tea." Then, realising that he should have made the same offer to the earlier caller, he added, "I can do that for you both." He was already at the French windows, taking off his Wellingtons.

The young fellow took her into the small dining room. He marched off to the kitchen and was still talking about tea, but Timberdick stayed on the mat until she had slipped off her shoes. "Please Miss, you don't want to worry about that. You know your sister. She can't be bothered with things like that. I took my boots off because they were awful."

"I'd die if I dirtied the carpet."

She walked into the middle of the large room. Here, tables and chairs didn't fight for position. Each piece of furniture stood in its own space. The carpet pile was thick beneath Timbers' toes and she played at flexing them as she walked, so that the woollen tufts tickled her. The walls were clean and pictures and mirrors hung in expensive frames. In the corner of the room was a cheval mirror. Oh, Timbers had always longed for one of these. If she had one, she would love it and love it. She had never been in a house like this.

But she sensed that things were wrong from the start. There were no photographs of the baby on the mantelpiece. No little toys to wave in front of him when he grizzled. And there was nowhere for him to be. No mat stowed behind the settee. No blankets folded on chairs or tucked beneath the dining table. And where was the changing basket?

The little one had not been here long enough for his mother to sort out her routine. In houses that Timbers knew, a new baby would lead to a mess. Here, the mess had been cleared away but the baby had yet to make his mark.

Still the youngster was talking. Mrs Thompson wouldn't be long, he said.

Timbers quietly walked up the stairs. The house was full of colours that she hadn't known during her own childhood. Soft shades that would look good only while they were fresh. But, in this house, they would always be fresh. He would grow up with a view of the world that, even now, Timbers couldn't recognise.

She walked into the nursery (and it was a nursery, not a bedroom) and realised that the little baby had been here for only a few days. Certainly not long enough to use powders, creams, towels and teats at different rates. No. Everything was just a few days old.

Susannah Thompson may be the infant's best chance of a good life – but she was living a lie. Timbers, so sure of her conclusion that she didn't have to spend time considering it further, thought about leaving by the front door while the young neighbour was still busy in the kitchen. But when she walked out of the nursery, she was surprised by a figure standing at the head of the staircase.

She was a pretty teenager with ebony hair and emerald eyes. Her cheeks that had a fine down, as if they had been coated like marshmallow."What are you doing here, Cynthia?"

"I didn't mean to come inside, but the little boy made it so easy. I only wanted to look at the house where my little brother was growing up. He is my half-brother, you know. I suppose that makes Mrs Thompson by step-mother, sort of."

"Cynthia, you'll cause trouble if you stay."

"Mind, I'd jolly well prefer her to my real mother. God, she's barmy."

Timbers took her into the nursery and said that they both had to leave, straightaway.

"I'm sorry I shot you. Scurries has explained that you were with him on the railway lines, so you couldn't have been Dad's mistress. I came up here just to see the house. I wasn't going to say anything, even if she turned up. It's nice inside isn't it? An awful lot of colours. Pale oranges and blues. And I like the stair carpet, a sort of rinsed russet. It's not like our place. Horrible, that's our place. Mum's got no idea of style."

Timbers made her sit down on the toy box while she sat cross-legged on the carpet. She didn't want to risk either of them being seen through the window.

"What are you going to call me?" Cynthia asked. "In the lower sixth – that's before I left, of course. I had to leave because of the trouble – they used to call me 'Hiya'. Do you get it? Hyacinth? Then when I got into trouble, the good ones came up with Cynful. Which I quite like, actually. It wasn't really 'trouble'. It was just because I knew how to flirt when the others didn't. I've always been able to pick-up older men, you see. Because of my sultry face. Do you think my face is sultry? People say it is. Because of the way my nose slopes and my eyes are deep green, almost emerald really, and sort of slanting and look down it. Rennie Tegg calls me Little Emerald Eyes. You know, I get such a buzz out of it. Knowing that I can make men feel like no-one else can. I mean, they're thirty and forty and even older, and they've wives at home and they've known hundreds of girls, I guess. But it's me that makes them feel a million dollars. Can you imagine it? Imagine how that feels?"

"I think it's best that we say nothing," Timber decided. "We should just walk out, through the front door, and not turn around until we get to the corner of the road."

"What do you think of Scurries? I mean, you did it with him?" The young woman sighed and crossed her hands in her lap. "You see, I haven't. I suppose I'm going to have to start thinking like a grown-up aren't I? No more silly tantrums and things. I get things in my head, that's the trouble. That's why I did, well, you know what I did from the Hoboken window. Listen, I've not told anyone this before, but I had an Everly Brothers l.p. and I wrote on it 'Dear Cynthia. With lots of Love Phil and Don.' I felt stupid because anyone could tell I'd written it, so I haven't shown anyone, but I promised myself – nothing else childish, since then."

"Cynthia, we cannot talk like this, here. We've got to get out of the way. I don't care about being caught in someone's house; it's the trouble we'll cause for other people."

"I love her fashion sense, don't you? I mean, those colours are going to be next year's colours and she's got them already. Gosh, it's awful to think that 1964 is almost over. Soon, we'll be in 1965. I wonder what that will bring. A new Beatles film, of course."

"I'm afraid it probably will. But we'll still worry about the atom bomb and blokes will be picturing what they're going to do in their last four minutes."

"Go abroad, me. That's what I'd do. What I thought was this. I mean

Scurries has made lots of promises but what I thought was this. Thirty-two pounds gets you a holiday in the Costa Brava. You fly. And Cherry Tegg says her Dad would pay for her. I mean, my old Doe's got no chance and, anyway, she wouldn't let me. (Do you get it? Old Doe? Mother deer – mother dear?) But if I had the money and said, listen you old bat, I'm going, 'ready-or-not', she couldn't do anything about it, could she? Which just leaves the thirty-two pounds and old fart Scurries. He says that he could find me a way of getting it. I mean, not doing anything dreadful. I mean, no one would touch me, he says."

Timberdick stood up. "Come on, we're going Cynthia."

The girl probably didn't realise that she hadn't listened to anything Timberdick had said since they had met at the top the stairs. She nodded, like a friend casually agreeing with another girl's choice of pop star, and followed Timbers' footsteps.

The lad was waiting for them at the bottom of the stairs, his gun belt around his waist and his six-shooter in his hand. "You're not Mrs Thompson's daughter," he said. "And you're not her niece. The ages don't fit. In fact, I don't think you've ever seen her before." He saw them thinking that his gun was a toy. It was made of a light alloy and had Wild West designs on the barrel. "This isn't real," he said. "But I've got to show you that I'm telling you what to do."

"You're right," agreed Timberdick. "We shouldn't be here and we'll do just as you say."

With a jerk of the pistol, he ushered them into the lounge. "Who are you?"

"Two friends," said Timbers. The girls were standing side by side on the hearthrug.

"I ought to search you."

"My friend's been watching me since I went upstairs," Timbers explained. "She's knows I have not taken anything. Ask her."

"But what about her? She went up first so you can't have been watching her."

Cynthia protested that she had no pockets.

"What were you doing there?" Timbers asked. "On the night of the train crash?"

"I was looking for you. I told you, I thought you were my dad's girlfriend."

The youngster listened without interrupting.

"Were you on the lines before the train came?"

"You know I was. That's when I saw Scurries and you."

"But I heard two people."

"Me and my Mum."

"Stop talking," he said. He told Timbers to hold the gun while he searched Cynthia. Seriously and politely and very decently, he checked inside her collar and the waistband of her skirt.

"She must have told you that I wasn't your Dad's girlfriend. I didn't know him."

"Yes, but I didn't believe her."

The boy nodded, satisfied. "You'd better go before Mrs Thompson gets back. We'd better not tell her that I let you in." At the front door, he added, "But she's lying. If you were with another man, she'd have known you weren't her Dad's girlfriend."

Nine

Timbers in the Bath

Timberdick promised herself this treat once every month but her life was so rarely free of interruptions that the four weeks often went by without her having enjoyed the indulgence to its completion. She put an extra bob in the meter two hours before she ran the bath, so that not only would the water be piping hot but the immersion heater in the little airing cupboard would be sufficiently fired up to warm her two best towels on the top shelf. Sadly, these towels were neither as white nor as fluffy as they had been when the eccentric gentleman had brought them for her, three years ago, but they were still better – and twice as large – as any towel that she could afford.

The flat was empty.

Doing things in the wrong order, of course, Timbers undressed on the bath mat then padded through the rooms to drop the latch on the front door, so that even if her old flatmates or Mrs Seaton turned up with a key, they wouldn't be able to get in. Then she came back, gathered up her clothes and carried them to her bedroom. She set the tea tray in her living room, leaving the kettle at the foot of the television table. She made sure that her favourite l.p. was on the turntable of the Dansette. Then she shut herself in the bathroom, locked it, and got the hot water going.

The tank held only enough water for one full bath. Timbers softened the water with three cubes, called 'Strawberry Peach from Cousins' and sat on the edge of the bath, picking at herself as the steam filled the room. Then, tip toes first and very carefully because, really, the bathwater was far too hot, she stood in. She bent her knees and for a long time was stuck with the water up to her shins and burning her. 'Oooh- ouch,' she sucked urgently as the hot water licked at

112

her tender white bottom. Then with a long, brave 'ou-ch' she lowered herself as completely as she could. She didn't move. She closed her eyes and when she opened them they were tacky. She let her ankles float to the surface and stretched out her arms. When she was satisfied that they had turned from white to lobster, and her cropped hair had been slickened by the steam and her perspiration, she began to talk to herself.

"Mrs S and Barbara Bellamy are two women with the best motives for murder." She knew they were at the scene, but where were they during the 'unknown minutes', those dark minutes when Donald Seaton was knifed in the neck and landed at her feet? And if either of those women did the murder, what would that mean for the baby?"

"The baby is Donald Seaton's, but he's dead. Plainly, Mrs Thompson isn't the real mother and the real mother doesn't want it. That means-" she waited as if for contradiction "-that means that Mrs S, as Donald's widow, has the best claim on the baby. The only honest claim."

Simple to prove, she thought. She lifted her foot from the water and puzzled over the shape of her toes that, she was sure, were becoming more crooked. You'd think that toes could live together, she mused, like children in a family, without squeezing. "Simple to prove. The things about my baby."

She didn't want to turn over because that would mean that her bath was half way finished, but her thinking had reached a stage that needed to turn a page. So, gently because the bath was very full, she rolled on to her tummy and, as if to tease although no-one was there to watch, let her buttocks come to the top so just a soapy trickle of bathwater ran between the cheeks. "And Donald Seaton's wife," she said, "is dotty about me." She dipped her chin and blew some bubbles. She wanted everything to be pink when she got out, her cheeks, her fingers, and her normally very white tummy. Laying on her front made sure that her breasts turned pink as well, something she loved to see. "So if I make sure the baby ends up with Mrs Seaton, I shall be able to be part of his little world." And she lowered her mouth, like a submarine, so that she could blow more bubbles.

Was that what it was about? Was she going to mess around with this tot's life, so that she could force her way into his life?

"No," she said out loud. "It's nothing to do with me." She was doing it because it was right. Every child deserves to know its own family. To be able to draw on its own background. To know its own truth. More than that; to have a past."

She lifted herself from the water. 'Like a lady born in the lake,' she said. (The Scotsman had said it, having paid to watch her; he was one of half a dozen clients who had been allowed in her home in seven years.) She wrapped herself in the two towels and, leaving the bathroom just as it was, went first to the living room where she got the record player and the kettle going.

The songs were from South Pacific. A world of sunsets, gentlemen and romance. She curled in the armchair, with a hot drink in her hands and her best white, cuddly, towel about her. And she told herself nice things about the world. Nice things, like words in the songs from South Pacific. She was going to make sure that 'her' baby had a start in life that she never had. She was going to make sure not only that Cynthia 'Cynful' Seaton didn't go to gaol for shooting at her, but also that the girl wouldn't end up disgraced in a bedroom at the Hoboken or selling her backside on the pavements of Goodladies Road. Cynful would see that life wasn't like liking good jazz. Good jazz comes twice only in dreams.

PART THREE

FRIDAY AND SATURDAY

Ten

Out in The Cold

The Volunteer was a thin pub for quiet men in brown suits and sober waistcoats. Here, a man could drink mild and smoke a pipe of clean tasting tobacco. The talk would be of football, the local greyhounds, cricket (in its place) but rarely of jump racing, no more than you would talk of America. Those things were too flamboyant for the men of the Volunteer. When these patrons had taken their suppers in their homes, at square tables with tartan cloths, their minds had already settled on stepping out for a drink while their wives put the children to bed. The wives looked forward to their ninety minutes alone with the wireless. It was 1964 and there was Vietnam, The Beatles and James Bond. England was swinging but, in my part of the city, populations lived this way in buttoned up streets until Radio Rediffusion and the last of the local breweries went out of business.

I had suggested The Volunteer because it was a steady walk from my rooms and there was little chance of being interrupted by someone from Goodladies. When I got there at eight, Len said, "He's upstairs. I'm to call him. Just the one night, he's booked in for. Who is he Ned, a commercial traveller?"

"A solicitor"

He went "Ooo" very quietly. "I'll mind my P's and Q's then."

George Hopley from Rother Street was sitting on a stool at the end of the counter. He took his pipe from his mouth, said "We ought to see you oftener, Ned," and put it back again.

"I'd like to get in more."

Another regular arrived and, seeing that the bar was unattended, sorted out sufficient coppers for a half, then waited patiently.

117

"You've heard about Miss Dorkings bit of bother?" Copley continued. "Left her purse on the kitchen table. She was in her front room for just two minutes and someone came through the back door and pinched it. She heard it, of course, but thought it was the woman from next door."

"Sounds like kids," I said

"No kids round here'd do it." Copley said surely.

"Kids on bikes," I suggested. "They'd come down the concrete path that runs along her back."

"Aye and away up to the embankment."

"I might check when I go home," I said.

"Be good if you did."

I liked Giles Unwin from the start. He was the picture of an understated Englishman from the thirties. He wore a brown suit and polished shoes of no more than sufficient quality and he was confident that a short back and sides would forever be the hallmark of good grooming. His chubbiness was turned into something stout and sturdy by an eight-button waistcoat, properly tied in at the back. You might think that he travelled in ties or leather goods, or was third in charge of a town's bank where he was trusted to bring on the young staff. But, I knew that Unwin had more gumption than any of these things suggested. He was the sort of man who preferred to be shorter than his wife; he was a resolute figure, slightly staid but no duffer. He was the sort of man that Scurries might have become, if Scurries hadn't got things in his head.

"I wanted to find you," he said as he shook my hand. "You called on my wife last year. You sat in the park and talked about her daughter." He bought a beer and we stepped across to a table at the back of the saloon. Giles Unwin had inquisitive nut-like eyes, hard but tawny, and a persistent nose like a beak that would keep tapping on things until it got the answer. But when he was thinking his face made no movement at all. It was a solicitor's face. It lacked the presence of a poker player's, but he was shrewd.

"I want to apologise Mr Unwin. I thought I could help, but when your wife spoke to me, I realised that I was meddling."

He nodded. "But without meddlesome intent." I waited while he enjoyed his first mouthful of beer. He had the knack of letting the flavour dry in his mouth. "Thank you for not exposing my lies. You knew that I had visited your city about ten years ago, looking for Billie. When I saw the life she was leading, I went back to her mother with a story that she had opened a dress shop and was buying a bungalow on the edge of the town. With that reassurance, she was happy to accept that Billie preferred not to meet her."

"But she's no longer happy with that?"

"Mr Machray, my wife died at the beginning of this year. Died, without being reunited with her daughter. Died, without Billie knowing where her mother was."

He accepted my sympathy with a courtesy that said I would learn no more about his grief.

"There is no money to come to Billie," he said frankly. "A solicitor weighs these things first, you may be thinking, but it is now nine months and matters need to be settled. Dundas and Taylor is a firm in the city centre."

I said that I knew them. They had been practising for three generations and were trusted.

"They will act on Billie's behalf when necessary. I am sure she is familiar with the magistrates' court, although I hope that her misbehaviour never bothers the assize."

I asked if I could help at all.

"Her mother was always content that you were keeping an eye on her. Perhaps you could continue, and ask Dundas to contact me if ever there's a need. You will understand, Mr Machray, I would prefer not to be bothered by these matters outside of the professional channels."

He was cutting himself off from his estranged stepdaughter. Gentlemanly, decently, thoroughly, even generously. But Giles Unwin was putting his past to bed and Timberdick now had no trail to follow.

He was half way down his beer, when he asked, "Does she need to know about these matters?"

"Timberdick never speaks of her mother," I replied. "And she doesn't know that we met."

"Yes," he said absently. "Timberdick. I've heard that you all call her that."

119

"I need to tell you, sir, that I asked Billie Elizabeth to marry me last Christmas.[7] She said no."

"Did my wife know about that?"

"No. It happened after we had talked. I want to assure you that nothing has ever happened between us."

"Good God, man. She's thirty-four. I'm sure I don't mind who she sleeps with." He lifted his glass. "You have my permission, if that's what you're after."

Later, Len told me that the man spent the rest of the evening in his room, asking for a sandwich to be taken up at ten o'clock.

I walked to Turks Street and found wise Susan playing hopscotch in the half-light. I asked where the boys from St Martin's School would keep their stolen goods. She knew that I was asking her because I thought she was a good and honest girl; that said something good about her parents and her parents would be proud of her. "You know you're only talking about Kemp and his brothers. None of the others do thieving. And you know they'd cut my gizzard out if they knew I was telling." Then she told me to look behind some loose brickwork in the old railway arch, "up from the foreshore, where we were throwing stones."

I wouldn't let her come with me. It was dark, windy and perishing cold by the water. I got as far as Lucy Lamey's make-shift garage, then picked my way through the twigs and brambles that had grown over the linesman's path. The ground was boggy and when, after more minutes than I had allowed for, I reached the old archway, mud was up to my ankles.

The place was pitch. I put both hands on the brickwork and felt my way along, past the first pillar, then counted three bricks back from the second. I dislodged a couple of bricks and found a shoebox of booty. I retrieved Miss Dorking's purse, but dropped some of the jewellery on the ground. I reached down for it, but I lost my bearings when I straightened up and knocked my head against the pillar.

I held myself steady until the dizziness cleared. And I had to sit down twice on my way back because I felt faint. The fuzziness wouldn't leave me for the rest of the evening.

---

[7]No fool like an old fool', the canteen ladies said.

I returned to The Volunteer before closing and handed the purse to landlord. "Don't mention where you got it from, Len." But I knew I would be invited to Miss Dorking's for tea and toasted scones before the end of the week.

* * *

When Fred Leaper beat on Timberdick's front door, Mrs S pretended that the house was empty. Then she peeped around the curtains and, realising that it was the man who ironed knickers, she lifted the latch and got him in quickly.

"Timbers won't be coming back," she said. "She's gone up The Nore Road and will be going straight on to work. You know where she works. That little bit of pavement opposite the Hoboken Arms. I thought I might stroll up there for a look. Now, you'd like a-"

"No," he said. "I haven't got time." Declining the offer of tea before it was properly made. "I need her to help me. The lads, they won't work with me."

"Then you certainly need a cuppa. Sit yourself down," she said. "You'll see that I've made little bits of changes."

He followed her to the kitchenette. "I don't understand. Do you belong here?"

Mrs S busied herself with things on the worktop. "Increasingly," she confided in an exaggerated whisper. "But not definitely."

"And Timberdick won't be coming back."

"Well, not until she's finished work. Now, what's this about the boys at work?"

She could find only one cup and saucer and that needed effort with the Brillo pad. (Really, Timberdick could be a dirty girl. It had to be said.) Fred Leaper had to manage with an ugly breakfast beaker. They went to the sittingroom where Mrs S stood on the hearthrug while the man made himself small in the armchair.

"They say that I'm too dangerous to work with. They say I panicked. Well, that wouldn't be so bad, but they know that I made up the story about the train falling over. Some of them say I even caused the crash, just to be a hero."

"I blame these Beatle people," said Mrs S. "They've got everyone thinking that they've got to be on tele."

"I was thinking that Timbers could tell them the truth. That she did all the work under the train and the story about it falling through the bridge was nothing to do with me."

"Have you met my daughter, Mr Leaper?"

"No. I mean, of course not." The question surprised him.

"She was there on the night and now, well, I don't where she is. If I'm honest, that's why I let you in the house. I thought you might have some news of her."

* * *

I was in a quiet mood as I began to walk home. I felt that I ought to seek out Timbers. Although I wouldn't tell her that her mother had died, it seemed proper that I should spend a few minutes with her. I had no idea what priests say at times like these but I thought I ought to try and do the same. I crossed the city and followed Three Beat past The Mechanics Arms and The Rose of Anjou. Then I stood on a street corner and tried to work out what I was going to say to her.

Timberdick was standing on her little bit of pavement in Goodladies Road, opposite the Hoboken Arms. It was a wet winter night, especially dark but mild. The cars made swooshing sounds on the rain soaked road and young women squealed playfully as they trotted along the pavements to the pub. Timbers was standing there because the drizzle had eased and she thought that men would want to pick up a girl quickly. This had been her pitch for years and her stick like figure was so familiar in the grainy picture that sometimes you didn't notice her when she was there and sometimes you thought she was there when she wasn't.

I watched from the shadows of Cardrew Street. I watched two cars crawl slowly past her. An older woman came out of her house and they talked for two or three minutes. Then Timbers was alone again, leaning against the brick wall in her short white raincoat and her stockings the colour of rich tea. I saw a young man, who looked like a clerk on a bicycle, stop to enquire but he didn't get off. Timbers stepped forward to encourage him but she looked bitchy rather than flirty. It wasn't her night for doing well. When the cyclist peddled away, Timbers looked along the kerb, eyes down, then looked up at the far off streetlamps and noticed me. She didn't make a signal. She turned her back and hurried down a side street. I followed, slowly, the ponderous plod of a lazy and overweight policeman. They were playing ragtime as I walked past the Hoboken. I heard Fat Tilly's shouting and the rude catcalls of old Mrs Wainwright. Doris Horsley saw us go past her window, first Timbers and then me. She was in a pink nightdress. She was watching Dragnet on a black and white television but keeping an eye on the road through a gap in the curtain. Likely story, she thought.

I thought that Timbers was heading for the stone porch of the old Methodist rooms but, at the last moment, she ran across the forecourt of Smithers' Motor Garage and broke through the loose panels in the fence. She wanted to lose me. By the time I got there, she had disappeared.

From the moment I had left Cardrew Avenue, I felt that I was being followed. So threatening was this sixth sense that, when I reached the church hall and saw no sign of Timbers, I ducked down a cobbled alley and lost myself in a web of uneven pavements, broken street lamps and dripping water. This was the rough part of 'Goodladies'. Out of sight of the road, I saw three children, less than ten years, squabbling over a game of dice. It was dark and their play was lit by the dirty yellow light from a scullery window. An upstairs window flew up and a woman called out to me. Did I know what I was about? Was I the man from Stockport who was looking for Number 23? From nowhere, a voice yelled at her to get back in her 'bouddi-warr'. Two toughs turned from the other end of the alley. Walking abreast, their fingers in their hip pockets and winkle pickers splayed, they forced me to stand up against the wall as they passed. (I wasn't in uniform. I was a fat man over fifty who shouldn't be out on his own.)

I emerged at another road and I was sure that a figure in a raincoat drew back into a doorway across the street.

A front door opened, not five yards to my left, and a squawking Baz Shipley spilled onto the pavement. She yelped in pain as the kerbstones cut her knees and she landed in the gutter. Her mother, in a fluffy dressing gown and soiled mules, stood on the threshold and gave her what for. The rude words rent the night sky. "Keep your drawers on, Old Mother Shipley," someone shouted from an upstairs window, somewhere. Another laughed loudly. A dog started barking and threw itself around a back yard at the end of the alley. I stepped back into the darkness.

When the front door slammed and the catcalls died away, the broken girl stepped into the alley and, not noticing me, sat on a concrete step. She had been dressed for a night out. Now, her stockings were ripped at the knees, beads of blood sticky on the nylon. Her make-up had been blotched by rubbed away tears and her hair was matted with dirt. When she saw me, leaning against the wooden fence on the other side of the alley, she said, "What you waiting for? You want a party?"

I said I was heading back to the Hoboken.

"Nothing there that you can't get here," she said. "What money you got?"

I asked if she was all right.

"Supposed to be going out, I was, bleddy cow. Look at me now. Can't go nowhere like this."

I offered her a handkerchief from my jacket pocket. "For your knee," I said.

"You got a wallet in there? Come on, you must have two or three quid for us. Thirty bob, then."

I produced my wallet, thinking that I could give her a ten shilling note.

"Bleddy cow," she said again, squeezing the flesh on her knee. "You're Ned, aren't you? Timbers bit of old fuzz." She had taken some minutes to recognise me out of uniform

"Well, yes."

"You've lost her. That's what you're doing here. She's given you the slip because she doesn't want you following her to the Side Roadhouse."

"Is that where she is?"

"Word is, she's rescuing her poor little rich girl. The girl who shot her." She looked at my puzzled face. "I can get you in," she said. "It'll cost you no money but you'd have to remember me and m'mum. If anything happens, one time." She understood my hesitation. "You need to think about it. The Side Roadhouse is nothing like the

Hoboken Arms. It's deadly dirty."

She led me through the back of Smithers' garage. We climbed the fire escape at the side of the old Hanworth flats, crossed the flat roofs and dropped down to the locked lorry parked behind the old mills. The guard and his dog recognised her filly-like figure as we emerged from the darkness and released the gate's padlock. (He thought that I was her client and avoided looking at me.) "There," she said quietly as we stopped on the top the footbridge that crossed the old train lines.

Side Road was terrace of uneven houses, abandoned by railway workers when the junction closed, fifty years before. The broken engines, prams, dustbins and timber crates that littered the no-through road didn't seem out of place. Every city needs a last place to go, just as a home needs a junk room or box cupboard, and the Side Roadhouse was a trio of three-storey houses where nobody came for any good reason. The windows were boarded up with ply and paint peeled from the doors and woodwork. The place looked dark and empty. No-one came and no-one went.

"Are you ready for this?" Baz Shipley warned, "Remember what I said; the Hoboken's for parties. A girl has to work hard in there."

Eleven

Working Hard

She told me to wait on the steps while she made a call from the telephone box at the end of the street. When I saw her walking back, I wanted to tell her that she didn't have to go in, but a man called Arnie was already coming out to meet us. She gave him money; a deal had been done. We went to the back of the houses, where he guided us through a dusty coalhouse and helped the agile Baz climb on to a low roof. "This time of night, the back way in's the best for the girls," he explained. "Come on, you and I will go through the engine room." He took me into a brick-built lean-to where a generator chugged and I had to crouch to avoid the sloping roof. (I didn't see Miss Shipley again.)

"Timbers' had a word. I've got to keep you out of the way of the business. Keep close and, for God's sake, don't touch any of the women. The one's that'll let you are already spoken for." We were inside the house. There were pictures of women on the walls and carpets (which made them strange to walk over) but none of them were real.

We reached the bottom of the stairs as two men in thick woollen overcoats were being let through the front door. The larger one looked me hard in the face and didn't like what he saw. "Copper," he said with just a touch of a snarl. "Are you sorting him out, Arnie?" His friend, an old man with no hair, a withered face and a frame that made him look like the butt in a comedy duo, said, "Make the bugger sweat for it, Arn."

Arnold pulled me along the passageway. "I'll show you where I work." He took me to the kitchen where tape recorders, spotlights and switches fought for space with an old cooker, kettles and crockery, a washing machine and even a wooden clothes horse. "I'm the projectionist when we run the films and I do the music and lights for the strippers." He punched open two serving hatches in the wall. "There's my auditorium," he said. It was a living room, much larger than you would have expected in this type of house. There was a leather settee and two upright armchairs and dining chairs stuck wherever a spare foot could be found. The makeshift stage was at the far end. It was three feet by eight, no larger. The girls had room to work with a hat stand or a single chair but a table or vanity suite as props were out of the question.

"Are your girls any good?" I asked.

"They better be. There's room for only eight gents in the audience. And they pay more than you earn in a week, so the birds better be chirpy." He went to the cutlery drawer and produced a dog-eared black and white photo. "She's on tonight. Scurries little girl. She'll go down well because she doesn't know what she's doing and the blokes'll know that. Makes her look like a virgin to them. She'll have them panting for more. 'Broken Hearted Melody' she wants to use. It's an old Woolworth's record by Maureen Evans. God, the trouble I had trying to splice that to make eight and a half minutes. That's what the boss says she has to do." Arnie was making tea as he spoke. Through the hatchway, I watched the withered man walk into the amateur auditorium and walk out again. Arnie handed me a mug of tea and left me, leaning my back against the kitchen sink, while he fiddled with the tape recorder. "Of course, you can only do so much with shitty kit like this. I'd love to have one of those new Grundig jobs. Professional outfits like they use at EMI. I suppose I fancy myself, really. I'd like to do a proper show in a proper theatre with a PA you can really do business with. Turn the lights out, Ed," he said. As I did so, he turned up the pianist's introduction to The Lady Is A Tramp.

In one's and two's they came, like reluctants called to prayer or cattle assembling at the farmer's gate. Some had cigars and one had a pipe and Old Withery had a whisky in his hands, although a notice said 'no drinks in here'. At first, they talked and then, when they were settled, they didn't. Then, they did nothing but wait. Frank Sinatra finished his song.

"You watch 'em," whispered Arnie. "Before the next track's done with, they'll be fidgeting like mucky schoolboys over a dirty mag."

A wave of nausea, brought on by the cigar smoke, reminded me that I had not yet properly recovered from my knock on my head. I steadied myself by gripping the Formica worktop.

"You OK pal?"

"Fine. Just a bit foggy round the ears."

"Get yourself an eyeful of Cynful in the raw," he said. "She'll soon put some colour back in your face."

She was standing on the stage, Mrs Seaton's daughter. Still, but wanting to fidget, with all the wariness of a girl called out to recite the homework she had not bothered to learn. She wore the skirt and sweater and white heels that Scurries had brought for her, just two days before. Around her neck, a white chiffon scarf. Around her waist, a broad plastic belt. She had placed a wicker shopping basket on the wooden chair. And a pink plastic dog on a plastic lead was at her side.

"Too sexy," Arnold commented in my ear. "I've told her. I've said tight skirts and jumpers give too much away too soon. Start plain, I said, but she won't listen."

"Shouldn't the tape have started?"

"Of course it bloody should've. I've told her not to come out until she hears the music. Christ, I've told her."

"She looks nice," I said and felt it was a soppy thing to say.

"I just hope she's washed her feet."

"Will this lot worry about her feet?"

"We were practising on the stage, earlier on. The boss said I had to coach her. More bump and grind and not so many smiles. I think she's got the hang of it. She ended up with everything off and treading on the dirty stage boards. I just hope she's washed her feet or the soles will be filthy."

"Yeah." I couldn't believe that anyone in the audience would be bothered.

"You can always tell a cheap stripper. Dirty soles."

Perhaps he meant souls.

At last the music started. Cynful stooped to stroke the puppy dog's nose, walked around the chair, then stood astride so that the toy, just three inches high, was looking up her skirt. The gentlemen liked the idea. Some laughed. Some clapped. But there was no cheering or hallowing her. The Side Roadhouse was, at least in one respect, a club for gentlemen.

The applause brought the young girl to life. She hitched up her skirt to show more of her stockings, turned around as she smoothed it over her bottom, then started to bump and grind with movements that were fighting talk. It didn't matter that every second had been tutored.

"Christ, get a move on. It's this crud music. It's too good. You can see her, wanting to dance to the bloody record instead of getting her clothes off. It's worse thing that can happen."

"What?"

"Getting to the end of the tape and there you are with your undies still on."

I didn't want to watch. When Arnie was diligently adjusting the lighting filters, I slipped out of the kitchen and found my way upstairs.

Something curious happened. The door at the top of the stairs was obviously a toilet door. I walked in and was about to occupy myself when I turned around and found young Fraser Stephens and a police dog standing behind me. He had been hiding in the room.

"Crike," I said, feeling stupid. "How many of you are here?"

He shook his worried head. "You mustn't tell. It's not like you think. Please, I've popped in to give Laddo a rest. I didn't know-"

"Of course, you didn't," I responded incredulously. "Why, no-one would have mentioned it to you."

"Please, don't give me away."

"Now then, what are you doing here?"

"Well, I don't know really, I'm supposed to be looking for Inspector Hillier. Boots and Hughes have been nicked in Lucy Lamey's car. They were racing it done the London Road. I think it might mean something. Think about it. They were driving in the wrong direction, weren't they? I want to tell the Inspector"

"You won't find our Jennie in a place like this," I said. "Her mother'd have kittens."

"No, I thought it was a bit mad. One of the probationers said. And

I said just what you've said – in a place like this? A strip club? That's why I came in uniform – in case I ever had to explain things to the Superintendent."

"And the dog?"

"I didn't come with the dog. He was outside and I recognised him and, well, we didn't really want to leave each other. It was like we both needed an accomplice."

"Stephens, I don't buy any of this. If you're going to do anything with a dog in a clip-joint, don't do it in uniform."

"Is that what it is?"

"You'd better get out, 'though God knows how. People might be suspicious of a police dog in a brothel."

"Oh God, is that what it is?"

"Oh yes," I muttered as I knelt down to scratch Laddo's neck. "It's definitely a police dog."

"I've seen Timberdick," he said. "I was thinking maybe she could help. Oh God, how have I got into this mess?"

"Where's she?"

"Along the landing, the door painted mustard."

"You had better lock yourself in," I said.

I walked out of the room and heard him lock the door behind me. If Stephens had been blessed with half a brain, I would have suspected that something more sinister was afoot. I had no doubt that he was up to something stupid, but I reconciled myself to growing no wiser.

Downstairs, men were applauding the best bits of Cynful's debut. Upstairs, things were going on behind the doors of different colours. But Timbers wasn't in the mustard room. At the end of the landing was a walk-in cupboard where beer crates were stacked against the wall. A plastic curtain separated it from the passageway. I heard Timbers' voice as I approached; I pulled back the curtain and caught her in business with a blonde sailor from overseas. She was holding her skirt up to her waist and leaning back against an old hand sink while he addressed her with his trousers and pants round his ankles. He had a dishcloth in his hand; probably, he had wiped her beforehand and wanted to wipe himself afterwards. Timbers saw me and pressed his face against her neck so she could mouth 'in the next room' with a toss of her head.

I stepped back, drew the curtain and walked unsteadily along the landing, holding on to the banister.

Cynful was sitting in the middle of men at the bottom of the staircase. She bubbled with enthusiasm. "As soon as I started to move, I knew that I'd got you. I knew I could make you do anything – catch your breath, lean forward. I could make your eyes twice as big as they were meant to be. Every time I looked along the front row, I could see that every one of you was uncomfy in your trousers and I knew that it was me who was doing it. I was just enjoying it so much. Then it got to the point in the tape where Arnie had played the song twice and joined it together and I thought, God, shit, we're half way through and all I've got off is my scarf and skirt. But it was just so, so good."

They let her get away with it, of course. She was young and new and every bit of naivety added to her value as an eventual prize. The eventual prize was, without doubt, what each of the men had in mind.

I waited in the mustard room with the light off. I had opened the curtains and was watching the street below. I wanted to know why I didn't despise my life in this city. Old moneyed men were fixing to take a young teenager to bed. My friend Timbers had sunk to doing it on landings where anyone could see. And, out there, schoolboys were making Sean take pictures of Django Rheinhardt from his shop window. I blamed the Beatles and the rest of these new people. But I blamed me for staying on.

I heard Timbers come in to the room but I didn't turn around.

"It's what I do, Ned. It's how I live,"

"Yes, but why out there? Why not in here? And the sort of man?"

"There is no sort of man, Ned. In my world every man's dirty in the head. Why else would they come fishing in muddy water?"

I let her know what I had been thinking at the window. "People will look back on these days and get them wrong. They'll talk about freshness, the revolution that money in the pocket can bring. Many will say that these are corrupt years where everyone wants to be famous or do shallow things because we might all be dead tomorrow. But how many people will remember the waste? We learned so much in the war and the years of chance that followed. Me, I was just watching from the sidelines. But that government we had, it promised so much. But all that we learned, we let lie fallow."

131

"Tomorrow we'll sell it off for silver," she said with such a prophetic tone that I thought she may have been quoting from the Bible.

"Maybe. Until then, we live in indulgent times. Like the rotting of Rome."

"Orgies, you mean?"

"Yes. Orgies of everything. Everything to excess."

"Come on, you soft plod, take your shirt off and we'll lay on the bed. You and me in the quiet."

"I don't think so."

"God, I'm not getting my legs apart for you. I'm saying let's spend some time together, that's all."

Then, I thought I heard her say, "I could. I mean, I could with my legs apart, if you wanted."

I turned to face her.

She shrugged and said, her eyes down, "I'd like to, that's all I'm saying."

The night in the brothel was the only time we made love. She didn't want it to be sexy, she said. She wanted it to be like two old friends who had found each other. Well, we were both old that night and a little beaten up by life. We got that right. She didn't want me to see her until she was undressed and in bed. That sounded silly because I had seen all she'd got to offer. The last time, just two minutes ago, behind the plastic curtain. But I played along. I avoided Fraser Stephen's toilet and went to the bathroom at the end of the passage and counted two minutes in my head. On my way back, the stray police dog brushed past me, without Fraser Stephens.

"Don't spoil it," she said as I walked into the bedroom. She meant, don't say anything. Holding Timbers' bare body next to mine was the sweetest thing I have tasted. I remember her smell; she came close with a natural earthiness, almost smokiness, like the scent of wet bark on trees. As if she washed all the time in rivers without soap. It made me think smell of fresh walnuts in a wooden bowl at Christmas. I pray that the odour comes back to me for my last moments on earth.

Afterwards, we sat up against the pillows and smoked two Park Drives. She wasn't going to marry me, she said, but I knew that already. I said I still wanted to run away with her and she said she wasn't going to do that either. Then she said we had better do it again because we might never get another night.

The second time was less smoochy but more playful. She teased me and made jokes about my body without saying a word. Timbers was good at sex.

"Curious," I said when we were sitting quietly again. I felt little fingers picking at the hairs on my thighs. "Hughes and Boots were arrested this evening for stealing Lucy Lamcy's roadster. Young Fraser Stephens has just told me in the bathroom. The curious thing is that they drove it all the way to Willersley Halt, then bought it back to the city. That's why they were caught. Because they were racing it down London Road. Now, if they'd made it back to the foreshore, I would have asked them how long it took. That'd be a nice piece of the jigsaw, you see."

"Yes, I can see that."

"You've worked it out as well?"

She said, "Fred Leaper was the only one who saw Barbara Bellamy trapped in the carriage. What if he's telling fibs? What if he arranged for the signals to stop the train at Willersley Halt, where Lucy collected Barbara in her car and they raced back to the station. Then she could have murdered Scaton on the bank. And Leaper gave her an alibi."

"Too complicated," I said.

She agreed but said nothing. We stayed still. Peacefully together.

"So, Hughes and Boots' joy ride was nothing to do with you, then?"

"Nothing at all," she said.

I looked up at the smoke rings I had been trying to puff in the air. "Power without responsibility," I said idly. "Kipling said it was the harlot's prerogative."

"He did 'Just So' stories, didn't he? I remember my Nan telling me some. Well, if he's saying that we never get the blame, he's bloody wrong. He should've stuck to elephants' noses."

I blew more curls of smoke towards the ceiling

She asked, quietly, "Can you get Barry Dundas to speak for them?"

"Stephens is already sorting it out."

She nudged me in the ribs. "Anyway, what's this? Telling me off after what we've just done?"

When I didn't respond, she asked seriously, "Did you get a good look at Cynful?"

"I didn't watch."

"But you heard them talking at the bottom of the stairs. You saw the look on her face. Ned, the kid doesn't stand a chance. She hardly knows what it is to be a woman and she's already decided that she's good at it. I've heard it so many times, Ned. The kid is hooked. To her, it's like liking good jazz. She'll want to do it again and again but she'll never recapture the buzz she's feeling tonight. So, she'll do other things. For nice blokes, to start off. But soon, she'll tell herself she doesn't care. There'll be the drink and the uppers, and two or three quid borrowed and she'll be on the streets trying to pay it off. She'll tell herself that she still has the power; that she's making the men feel uncomfy, that she can make them do just as she wants. God, I tell myself that, don't I, after all these years? But there's one power she hasn't got. The power to stop. It starts here, Ned."

"There's nothing we can do about it."

"Someone's got to help her. Her bloody mother's got no idea."

"It's not your fault, Timbers."

"Bloody Scurries, I'm sure he's to blame. He went off with her after the shooting and she's ended up here. How'd he do it, Ned. Who does he know?"

"It's like liking good jazz, you said?"

"That's what her father called it. He said that the first time you hear good jazz, it excites you so much that you carry on looking for the same thrill. Of course, you never find it, because it's never the first time again."

"Yes."

"So what was the first time for you?" she asked. (It was very unusual for Timbers to ask about my likes and wants.)

I was looking up at the ceiling. "That's No Bargain, by Red Nichols and The Redheads. It would have to be the Perfect Records version; they are others, on Brunswick and Vocalion, but they're not so good. It starts very quietly, you see. Tame, I suppose. A bit sedate, like a horse walking around the parade ring before the race." Then I remembered Annette Hanshaw's Black Bottom. "But that's a cheat because the thrill is Red Nichols' solo. No, it'd have to be Jack Teagarden's I've Got A Right to Sing The Blues. You know I can remember when I first heard it."

She laid a hand against my ribs. "Really, Neddie. That's enough. The title would have done. We're talking about Cynful, remember?"

"I keep going back to it, but not to recapture the magic. It's different for me. It's like returning to a favourite pipe or familiar slippers."

She pressed her hand a little harder. "Really, that'll do. I was only asking."

I said again, "There's nothing we can do about Cynful."

"We could get her out of here for a start."

"Not without causing a riot."

"You do realise what they're going to do with her, don't you? They were bidding for her on the stairs, a bloody auction. And when they've flattered enough, they're going to bring her to an upstairs room and take turns. Three of them. One, while the other two watch."

"Timbs, there's nothing we can do."

"Perhaps if someone had said something different twenty years ago, I wouldn't have worked on street corners for half my life."

"You've not met Fraser Stephens. A young copper, still wet behind the ears. He's turned up here in uniform."

"Baz," Timbers guessed. "She said she had something lined up in costume."

"But he found a police dog outside."

"That's more like 'Slowly' Barnes. She likes to tie blokes up and get dogs to sniff at them, or cats to leave their smell all over them. God, I hope he's strong. You know 'Slowly', she'll have him for breakfast."

"But what would a police dog be doing outside a brothel?"

Two fists pounded on the door. "Let me in! Open up you two."

Timbers and I recognised the voice. "The door's open," we said, almost together.

Inspector Hillier, curiously dressed in a bell-bottomed sailor suit complete with a square neckerchief, strode into the room. "This is a raid!"

"Don't be silly, Jen," I countered. "You can't arrest us – we're your friends."

"You pair of dopes, I'm not doing the raiding. Fraser says the word's out. They're bringing vans and dogs and half my class of probationers. I want you to hide me."

I asked, "You mean you're here, not on duty?"

Timbers was quick to stall any reply. "You frisky cow. Baz said she had some fanny in one of the rooms. My God, don't you ever think of bloody pinching me on the street, Jennifer Hillier."

"Ned," Jennie pleaded. She was bobbing from one leg to another, like a child who needs the toilet.

"Where's Cynful?" I asked.

"Cynful?" She looked anxiously over her shoulder. "Ned, hide me."

"Where's the bloody stripper, woman," persisted Timberdick.

"Oh. Oh, she's across the way."

I got to my feet. "Right, come one, Jennie. We're going to make some arrests."

Our assault on the room with the sky blue door is one of the most vivid memories of my friendship with Timberdick and the girls. At the time, our fun was tempered by an awareness that if our uniformed colleagues interrupted us too soon, Jennie and I might be sacked and Timbers would spend the night in a chilly cell. But, years later, I can recall it all with a chuckle and every time I do I recognise some new detail or nuance. The memory is like an old movie that gets better every time.

Inspector Jennie took the lead. She was in her navy kit and Timbers wore some man's top. God alone knew where the owner was or the rest of Timbers' clothes. But the shirt-tails were long and she looked like a nursery drawing of Wee Willie Winkie. So when we marched across the passageway, we looked like the fancy dress parade on the endpapers of a children's annual.

"Open up!" Jennie said.

"In the name of the law," Timbers added.

I opened the door (it wasn't locked) and we all trooped in.

Looking back, it worked well. Timbers played 'informer' and, as soon as we were in the room, rushed to wrap her arms around the teenager. Jen stood as pompous as only Jen can, and announced her arrest of two men in underpants and Scurries in his corset.

Timbers identified the phoney doctor and a pretend army officer who had approached her downstairs. Scurries was the prettiest. His white corset was not just dainty, with lace frills, silk bows and buttons, it was a quality garment that, pulled tight, trimmed his figure and made a more masculine shape of his spotty shoulders. The Major was one of those fatties who raise their waistline by twelve inches so that the elastic of their underpants fit beneath their plump bosoms. But the make-believe doctor was disappointing. His briefs sagged and appeared to hold nothing of substance. He was the one who looked like he wanted to argue.

The girl had her clothes on but the liveliness had drained from her face. She stood pigeon-toed, with her fingers interlocked on her belly. She looked intimidated by so much white flesh but her anxious stance did not weaken her look of careful resolution. I did not know what had been going on in the room, but Cynful had stood up for herself.

"You are all under arrest," Jennie kept saying.

No-one protested.

"The girl is under age," she declared.

Cynful, realising that a rescue was afoot, confirmed, "I am only fourteen."

The three stood still, mouths open. Cynful was a mature sixteen years old. She could not possibly have been fourteen. No-one believed it. So, to extinguish any doubt that a Police Inspector's truth cannot be denied, Jennie proclaimed, "I am Inspector Hillier of Shooter's Grove Training Centre. I am on Special Duties."

Timbers had walked behind the man she had first met at the top of Moore's Lane and began to tug at the lace trim of his corset. "This – is a corset."

"It's not a lady's," he insisted. "I have it specially made. I'm not wearing ladies' clothes, honestly."

"Honestly or dishonestly, you are wearing a corset from Bellamy's on the Nore Road."

"You're all under arrest, every one of you." Jennifer declared. "Ned, line them up against the wall."

"We can't do it," said Timberdick. "We can't arrest them without explaining what you two are doing here. And," she cast a big sister's eye at Cynful. "I don't want to get this stupid Daisy in trouble."

"Lock the doors!" Jennie ordered.

"The doors don't lock, you know that."

"Then there's no time to lose. We'll have to leave by the window."

"Oh, wake up Jen," Timbers protested. "There are police dogs down there, waiting for worried men and wayward girls to run away. We need decoys."

We all looked at the men in pants.

"Right! Get dressed!"

"They'd be better in white underpants. They'd be seen in the dark."

Now, the Major stepped forward. "Ladies, look here. You've caught us in a dizzy situation. We are...er...at your disposal to a certain extent, yes. But there are bounds."

Timbers allowed Inspector Jennie no time to consider the appeal. She pointed to the phoney doctor. "You first."

It was time for me to speak up. I knew that Timbers wasn't going to allow any of them to escape with their Y-fronts. It was a cold and wet night out there and jumping from a first floor window isn't good exercise for any man without his dignity. "Just a minute, Timbers. Where's the noise? If this house is being raided, it's the quietest posse of coppers I've known."

Jennie said, "Fraser said."

"Said what?"

"Said we should get out if we didn't want to be caught in a raid." She thought a little and said, "The snivelling bastard."

"He wanted to scare us off," I said.

"He wants to tuck himself up with some lipsticked floosie, I shouldn't wonder. There never was a raid, was there?"

Then we heard the screech of a policeman's whistle. A dog barked and a woman screamed.

"Christ," said Jennie, her teeth clutching her bottom lip. "Ned, we're in for it now."

"Timbers, get the girl out of here," I instructed. "Jennie, scarper. Just scarper."

"No. No, I want to look after Bazzie."

Leaving the Inspector to her desires, I tried to shuffle Cynthia and Timbers through the bedroom door. "What about the men?" the girl said.

I said they could look after themselves.

But Timbers hadn't finished with the Man from Scurries. With two fingertips, she twisted the hair at his temples until he sat down on the carpet. Then she put her mouth close his ear and, keeping him still with her knee against his neck, whispered, "You won't get away with the train crash, Fat-Mouse. You've lost your job and your family won't know you and you'll live the rest of your life alone, dreading the knock on your door. You want to say sorry, don't you?"

He nodded and mumbled 'yes' only as loud as she allowed. He was making a noise at the back of his throat, like a child trying not to cry.

"Well, I won't let you say sorry. I'll make sure that they never find you. You'll never get the chance of a rest from the worry." Her voice was full of nastiness. "Think on, Fat-Mouse. Think on what you were going to do to this girl. And know that Timberdick stopped you."

I had expected to find pandemonium in the passageway, but there was only a sexily dressed nurse, carrying armfuls of toilet tissue to the room with the crimson door. I led Timbers and Cynth to the stairhead.

"I'm confused," muttered the teenager. "I thought it was a raid."

"No, just Fraser blowing his whistle."

I found him in a room of crimson veils and scented candles. The woman in her forties was dressed in red. Red negligee, red lingerie, red ribbons and bangles. She sat on a bed of cushions and held her knees up to her chin so that he Naughty Night Nurse could wrap toilet tissue around her injured ankle.

"Bloody dog!" she spat. "Bloody bit me. He'd sniff, that was the bargain. Bloody sniff, that's all." Her eyes had yellow streaks and ointment seeped over the raw edges of the eyelids.

Young Fraser Stephens was standing in the corner. He was wearing his helmet, his boots and socks and nothing else. He held his truncheon erect in one hand and his whistle on a chain in the other. When I spoke to him, he put his fingers in his mouth and gibbered.

"Laddo?" I asked. "You found him on the street?"

"Did he, buggery?" laughed with the woman with sickly eyes. "He's been on at me for days, wanting to come here in his uniform with a dog and I'd let him arrest me. That's what he wanted. The dog would have to search me, he said. And like a bloody old whore, I said yes. O.K., I said. Get on with it, I said. And the bloody dog's bitten me."

The nurse comforted her. "I've called my Chief Inspector," she said. "He's coming to get him."

That's what persuaded me to leave.

Twelve

The Early Turn

I got to the police station at half past five. I had decided to report for duty that night, having taken five days sick leave. I was late, but expected to do nothing more than cook breakfasts for the lads. I knew something was wrong when the Superintendent followed me into the toilets. Officers-in-Charge have their own. While I was busy, he checked the cubicles for cleanliness then stood at the gallery of sinks and soaped his hands like Lady Macbeth.

"Where were you last night?" he demanded.

"Where was I?" I asked as I got to the next washbasin.

"I was in here for two hours and no-one could find you."

"Sir, surely not. Waiting for me in the ablutions for two hours?"

"Not 'here – the gents'. 'Here – on duty'. I've decided that we can do without you."

I didn't like the determined set of his face.

"You can't sack me," I said. "Not without proper procedures."

"I'll do what I like," he asserted. "You want a proper hearing? Lord, I'd have a field day. Anyway, I'm posting you to a rural division. You can sleep there and no-one will notice." He stood in the middle of the floor and shook his hands dry. "Follow."

We were alone on the fifth floor of the police station. There could not have been half a dozen others in the building for the night turn had yet to come in at the end of their shift. As I walked along the carpeted corridor to the Super's office, I warmed to the idea of retiring to the country. It offered a sense of rounding off my career in a comfortable, pastoral way.

We stepped into his room. A desk lamp was the only light and my personal file was open on his desk. We didn't sit down.

"Tell me about your war?" he asked, leafing through my papers.

"My war, Sir?"

"What is it with you, Machray? Why do you answer everything I say with another question?"

"I'm sorry, Sir. It's just – I suppose I'm having trouble keeping up."

"Yes," he concurred. "I can't understand why we're doing this." He looked up from the folder. "What did you do in the war?"

"Lorries, Sir. Mainly. I offered advice on road haulage."

That told him nothing, of course. "Yes, well I understand if it has to be 'hush'. Well, you've certainly got some friends in the world of secrets and subterfuge. The Chief Constable's had to agree to your transfer to the moors."

I began to feel uneasy. "People have asked for me to move? I mean, it's not a disciplinary measure, after all?"

"Hardly a punishment, Machray. Feeding nibbles to moorland ponies and stopping country folk having babies in the woods."

I fidgeted. "Look, I'm not sure about this."

"Too late, I'm afraid, Machray. It's out of our hands."

"Sir, you don't understand. If these people have got things in mind for me, God, I'll end up breaking into depots and stowing away beneath tarpaulins. I'm too old for it."

"Out of our hands, Machray. The Chief Constable has agreed to your transfer."

"He can't have."

"Don't be daft, man. The Chief agrees to whatever he wants."

"Look, I've been thinking. You're quite right, I've not been pulling my weight recently."

"Recently?"

"I could do a lot more in this division, Sir. I've got ideas."

"PC Machray, you don't belong to this division anymore. Take your ideas to the moors. That's where we're sending you."

"When do I start?"

"That's none too certain." He consulted the papers again. "At once, it says. But my notice doesn't assign you to a particular station." He made a shape with his mouth. "Divisional Headquarters, I suppose. But I can't give you a time to report."

"That's because I won't get there, Sir. I'll be picked up on the way.

Sir, you don't understand how these people work. By tomorrow night, I could be hiding in a ditch with my face blackened and a commando knife in my belt. God, Sir, I'm over seventeen stones. I haven't got the shape for it and I'm too old."

* * *

At a quarter to seven in the morning, Billie Elizabeth 'Timberdick' Woodcock, a 34 year old prostitute who had run away at fifteen and was beginning to think about God but probably not, because she had worn no knickers since six o'clock the previous evening, climbed onto the coal bunker at the back of Bellamy's haberdashery and forced the pantry window. Baz had done borstal for burglary and had taught Timbers so many tricks of the trade that she could break in with the confidence of an experienced crackswoman. As she clambered through the small window and landed on the large white refrigerator, she was careful to leave the way clear for a hurried escape. She left the windows and doors open so that she didn't need to switch on a light. A change in temperature, she had been told, was more likely to disturb someone's sleep than a familiar light downstairs. Barbara would dismiss a light as her own carelessness, she would be more curious about an unexplained coldness. And Timbers didn't want the lady upstairs to stay in bed during the trespass. Indeed, she needed to wake the cow.

Timberdick filled three buckets and bowls with cold water and set them at the foot of the stairs. She considered this arsenal, then found a crate of empty milk bottles and three two-pint jugs that she charged in the same way. Then she moved about the shop floor. She took sunglasses from the counter display and snapped all the handles. She opened the hosiery drawers, unwrapped four pairs of stockings so that she could poke her fingers through. Then she went to a stock rail and popped the buttons from three soft cloth jackets. Looking for more mischief, she crouched behind the counter and discovered a box of ledgers and invoices. She ripped the pages from the books and scattered the papers across the floor. She turned a brief case upside down and threw a file of estate papers in the air. (These were Donald and Barbara's dealings with the shop deeds.) Now that she knew who was to blame, she allowed every ounce of spite to get the better of her behaviour. She broke the woman's cigarettes in half and tore the serial numbers from ten shilling notes in the petty cash. She would have done more damage, but she heard Barbara moving about upstairs. Timbers got ready with the first bucket of water.

Come down, she thought. Come down in your dressing gown and see why it's so cold.

Bleary eyed and unsteady on her feet, Barbara Bellamy descended a step at a time. She gripped the handrail with one set of fingertips and held her nightie above her ankles with the other. She saw no-one. She put her toes on the bottom step and a cannon ball of water hit her face. She fell back, gasping for breath, her hands at her face trying to clear the stuff from her eyes. Then, before she had chance to say anything or clamber upright, another wave sent her sprawling backwards. Her nightclothes and her hair were drenched.

"You bitch!" an unfamiliar voice shouted from somewhere sideways.

She tried to support herself on her elbows, but yelled when she saw the third bucketful coming. It hit with her mouth open and turned her, choking, onto her knees. Now, she couldn't draw air into her lungs; she began to panic.

"You told Scurries about Cynthia Seaton! He was here, buying his corsets, and set the young girl up. You told him to get her on stage at the strip club."

Still on her knees, still hurting, Barbara Bellamy knew what was happening. "It's you. Please, give me a moment."

But Timbers had the first of the bowls ready.

"No!"

The water shot into Barbara's face again. She thumped and stamped in temper and another bowlful came, as if to discipline her for her truculence. She whimpered, "Please."

Timbers picked up two milk bottles and hovered.

"Please. I've done nothing wrong."

"She hardly grown, for pity's sake."

"Please. A minute or two, that's all." She sat on the stairs with her knees apart and her face down. Spluttering, sucking in breath and snorting. She rubbed her eyes with the backs of her hands and used fingers to comb her dripping hair. Her dressing gown and nightie were out of shape and see-through.

Timbers stepped forward. "Why?"

"No!" Barbara lifted a hand. "No, don't ask questions. You'll only get cross again. Please, I'll tell you."

"Do you want to drink?"

"Yes." But the shopkeeper didn't trust her tormentor. She kept her hand on guard as Timbers handed over the bottle of water. Barbara sipped, two or three times and, knowing that she had to behave, gave the bottle back. "I'm cold," she said.

"You're bound to be," Timbers conceded uncaringly. "What with the water and hardly any clothes on. There's more to come."

"For Chris'sake, Timbers. What's this for?"

"Who killed Donald Seaton?"

"Honest to God, I don't know. Look, I'd done everything for Donald. You know that I lived with his baby, here in the shop, for months. His mother wasn't able to cope, he said. So I said, of course Donald, I'll even move in here so that my neighbours won't ask any questions and I'll look after the child you had with another woman."

"How did the baby get to the old railway carriage?"

Barbara didn't know. "Ask his mother. He was with her that day, not me."

"So what were you doing in London?"

"You know. Glenys has told you that we were trying to sell the shop. But things didn't go according to plan. Donald wanted to be greedy, as usual. That led to an argument and we even sat in different coaches on the way back."

"So you weren't friends, in the end?"

"Of course, we were. And we'd have been lovers again, if it wasn't for his daughter. Cynthia got in the way of Donald taking me back. Her mum would have put up with our affair, but Cynthia kept telling her to stand up for herself. Then she started to say things to her dad, making him feel guilty. Was it anything to do with her, if Donnie and I were happy?"

"So you gave her up to Scurries."

"Not like that."

"But you knew what Scurries would do to her."

"I'm not sure about that. Scurries had plenty of reason to want revenge. Donald had found out about his corset-thing. Come on, we were having an affair and we had most of it upstairs in the stockroom. Donald found the packs of corsets, like you did, and he started to tease Scurries."

"Blackmail?"

"No. It was Scurries' idea. He was eager to buy Donald off but, after all these months, I'm not surprised he wanted to get his own back. Cynthia was just the easiest way of doing it."

Timbers put one foot on the bottom step and reached forward until she was holding the bottle of water above Barbara's head. The woman's hands went up, clutching at Timbers' outstretched wrist. "For Heaven's sake, Timbers! That's enough!"

"What did you expect him to do to her?"

"She wanted to strip off for an audience, didn't she? Go on, tell me she didn't want to do it!"

"You knew what they'd do to her."

"That's nothing to do with me."

Timbers tipped the bottle and the water streamed down Barbara's forehead. The woman had learned not to fight. She took it like a practised victim of the school bully. She made bubbling noises until the water had gone. "O.K. I suppose I knew they'd make her do other things. I wanted the girl to go through it, didn't I?"

Timberdick withdrew. She picked up another bowl of water. Two jugs and more bottles remained ready at her feet.

Timbers threw the water. This time, Barbara got to her feet. Perhaps she lunged forward to protect herself. Maybe, she wanted to push Timbers out of the way. Timbers kneed her belly. Barbara fell forward, sending Timberdick backwards. Both women slipped on the floor and Timbers felt her head crack against the mahogany shop-counter

* * *

Inspector Jennifer would have preferred to wash before turning up at the Superintendent's room on the fifth floor. The ACC had already hinted that her recall to CID was imminent and she was sure that the note in her pigeonhole – asking her to report to Room 501 – was the start of that rehabilitation. But she was pressed for time. Baz was a naughty girl who encouraged decent girls to be lazy. She made the little room in the Side Roadhouse seductively decadent. So, Jen had indulged herself with an early morning breakfast in bed, having been teased about her old fashioned underwear, betting about what she could and couldn't reach when she was undressed and looking for her clothes – all these things held her back from getting home, changed and ready for work. Ten minutes in the locker room loo put her clothes straight and tidied her hair, (though it refused to lay in the way it naturally did) but Jen didn't have time for a strip wash and her arms and legs felt sticky where they joined the rest of her. And her blouse wasn't her best. She fidgeted with it as she walked into the Superintendent's office; she was sure it didn't fit her like it used to do. Damnation! It wasn't hers; she must have picked someone else's from the Training School's laundry by mistake.

"Please remain standing," said the Super. "I have a couple of points to discuss." His voice was clipped and taut; it didn't sound like a welcome back to the operational front line. He sat squarely behind the desk, picked up a freshly sharpened pencil and held it between two thumbs and forefingers, as if he were testing its resistance before snapping. "Constable Stephens believes he saw you at the Hoboken affray."

"He can't have done, Sir. I wasn't there," fibbed Jennie.

A confident liar, judged her superior officer, but not very good.

She tried to smarten herself up; she brought her heels together and kept her arms flat at her sides, without expression. She wasn't quite standing to attention but she looked like an Inspector on the carpet.

"He seems very sure."

"He's mistaken, Sir."

He brought a manila folder from his in tray. "Well, we have these," he said, producing more than a dozen photographs from the file. "Taken less than six hours ago, Miss Hillier."

Jennie wanted to hold on to something. Why did bossy men never invite her to sit down when she needed to? As she watched the Superintendent spread the endless series of black and white pictures across the desktop, Jennie rubbed a finger across her left eye.

(Something she hadn't done for a long time.)

They were upside down to her, of course, but the images of Baz and Jennie in bed didn't need to be the right way up.

"Who took them?" she asked.

The Superintendent smiled unworthily – he felt a superior smugness that The Force had been too clever for this woman.

She secretly dug her nails into the palms of her hands and clenched her toes in the polished caps of her policewoman's shoes.

"Oh," he said indulgently. (He must have been a really horrid little boy, she thought.) "Oh, we have a spy in the camp, don't you know. An agent working undercover."

"Of course," she said. Then she recognised her own excuse. "Of course, that's what I was doing. Working undercover."

"Of course. That's what we hoped you'd say. Unfortunately working undercover without authority is undesirable, Inspector. And that makes you, Inspector Hillier, an undesirable Inspector." He sighed, gathered the pictures together in pile and put them away for later. "I believe you need improved supervision. I have asked Chief Inspector Wren to assign you duties that will afford this. It will mean a posting, a new job, but – believe me – a new job in my division. I will not be letting you out of my clutches. I am determined, Miss Hillier, that you will hate every moment you work under me. I blame you for the coming to grief of young Fraser Stephens. I don't know what you had to do with his liaisons last night, but I blame you. Do you know where my secret policeman found him?"

"Sir, no. Sir."

"In uniform!" he shouted and thumped the desk so that photographs bounced. "A young and promising probationer, now fallen into vice and imperilment."

"Imperilment, Sir?"

"In uniform and he said he was looking for you. (He had another woman in his arms when he said it, I add) You – you are a disgrace. A filthy, loose-living, cheap-thinking and smutty disgrace. So, I have decided to move you to Schools Liaison. You can take charge of the lollipop patrols."

"Yes, sir. I'll lick them into shape."

The Superintendent's head jerked with an involuntary grunt.

"Don't poke fun at me, my woman."

Jennie felt colour come to her face.

"Besides, the laugh's on you. We're short of lollipops so you will have to undertake many of the patrols yourself. West Street Primary is a good one, I'm told. Early mornings, dinners and home time, I'll expect to see you on the railings."

"Yes, Sir."

"I have promoted 'Stand-by' Moreton to Sergeant and he will head the Shooter's Grove Training School."

"A Sergeant? I thought it had to be an Inspector." Jennie felt the reduction in her old post more keenly than the six months fatigues at the school railings.

"Yes, yes. The A.C.C. may insist that I temporarily promote him to Inspector. So be it. We need to recognise the work that Stand-by has done for the community in Goodladies. He has revolutionised this Constabulary's approach to dog litter. The Chief describes him as a worthy ambassador. Vision. He has vision. Do you know, Tommy believes that a day will come when people will have to pick up their dog mess from the pavements and take it away with them. Quite, quite, visionary. He will do well at Shooter's Grove, plainly. He will bring discipline to the place. Good Lord, have you read the immersion bill?"

"Bill, sir?"

"The water heater. Good God, woman, what have you been doing. Bathing in it! And, you were supposed to have special responsibility for WPC's on probation." He paused, tapping his fingertips on the table. "Miss Hillier, I've heard stories about irregularly clothing."

"Sir, that's not fair. I told Chief Inspector Wren about that and he told me not to get into it."

"I'm talking about erotic underwear." He emphasised, "Shared erotic underwear."

"Yes, sir."

"Well, perhaps Mr Wren saw things that I didn't." He selected a picture of Jen and Baz Shipley kissing. "Is there a man who can keep you interested, do you think? People tell me that you've taken a shine to old Ned Machray. I'm told he used to look after you when you first joined the force."

"He's very old, Sir."

"Fifty-four, Miss Hillier. Not especially old. I'm told a man can look quite distinguished at fifty-four." He adjusted the tufts of grey hair at his temple.

"They can, Sir."

"Your diary, Miss Hillier."

"My diary, Sir?"

"You lost it last year and it turned up in the policewomen's W.C. Someone passed it to me and, believing that you would be very embarrassed, I threw it away."

"Oh, thank you, Sir."

I could hardly help seeing, just a scribble or two of it. I was tearing it up, page by page, as I stood over the toilet, you understand."

"Thank you, Sir."

"And P.C. Machray's name – Ned – seemed to catch my eye quite a bit."

"I did think about him, quite a bit at the time but-"

The Superintendent cocked an eye.

"I knew I was safe with him. I didn't want a man who would have expectations of me and, well, Ned wouldn't expect anything like that, would he?"

Horror cast its darkness over the Superintendent's face. "Grief woman, what do you mean? You mean he's another one?"

"Oh no, Sir. That would be unfair to you."

"And to the station, Miss Hillier! Oh, 'how is the faithful city become a harlot. Righteousness lodged in it, but now murderers'"

"I don't think you can call PC Machray a murderer, Sir."

"I was quoting from the Bible, Miss Hillier. I believe."

"It's just, he likes a particular type of woman. Not me."

"I don't suppose he could be persuaded...it's your welfare, I'm thinking about."

"Sir, I won't be seeing Miss Shipley again. If you want me to promise that, I will. There's no need to appoint anyone to distract me."

"I'm afraid there is another matter," he said. "DC Furrows' complaint."

"Constable Furrows, Sir?" She wanted to emphasise Furrows' lowly status.

150

"He says that you telephoned an alert that we were about to endure a race riot."

"I don't think I said 'race riot', Sir. And it was hardly an 'alert'. I was passing information."

The Superintendent conceded her point with a dip of his head. "Information that some leather jacketed lay-abouts were dissatisfied with the state of an old man's peas."

"Sir, there were incidents."

"Inspector, there was no incident. I have checked the log myself. My sub-division has suffered no civil disorder. Neither has any part of the city."

"Sir."

"I have been careful to check thoroughly, Inspector." He stood up and walked around the desk. Jennie sharpened her stance. Now, she was standing to attention. "My predecessor," he began.

"The Superintendent? Yes, Sir?"

"He had problems with you? He made you stand in his office on one occasion?"

"Yes, Sir. Sir, that was in my diary too, Sir."

"I just wanted to reassure you."

Jennie stopped his progress. "Sir, I am reassured."

"Yes. Surely. But I can't have my operational Inspectors panicking every time some ton-up lad picks his nose."

"Hardly panic, Sir."

"You know, Mr Wren is very disappointed; he was expecting promotion this year but your activities under covers have scuppered those hopes. Now," Here, he inhaled deeply through his nose. "Ah yes, now, we need to keep you occupied. A van is leaving for South Withers in a few minutes. You will be on that van. They are moving the police station and will need a hand. You'll be no good at lifting furniture, I suppose, but you can brew tea and cut sandwiches. Good day, Inspector."

"Sir?"

"I said, good day, Inspector."

"No, sir?"

"Miss?"

"The photo's, Sir. I couldn't have them, could I? I would feel much better if I could."

The Superintendent considered. What would the girl want with them? Destroy them? He suspected not. Drool over them on lonely winter nights? No, Inspector Jennifer was not the drooling type. Perhaps she wanted to keep them as a memento of her one sordid evening.

"Are they evidence?" he asked. "Do they provide a clue?" He was gently mocking but he also needed reassurance. "You're not working on a case, Inspector? A private case? I have the negatives, of course."

"You do, Sir."

He shrugged, tucked the flap inside the folder and handed the bawdy archive across the desk.

* * *

Timberdick came to slowly. She felt whoosie; she guessed that she would lose her balance if she moved quickly. Dust from the wooden floorboards troubled her throat and nostrils and every cough made the blood pulse heavily at the back of her head. The flesh felt so heavy there that she checked with her fingertips for swelling. Papers that she had thrown from the shop files were wet now and stuck to her arms and legs like licked tickets. She pulled a flimsy square of paper from her knees and, because it stuck to her fingers, brought it close to her face. It was the carbon of a receipt from a south London garage – the name of the purchaser made her examine it closely. It was a receipt made out to Donald Seaton for a Riley 1.5 Roadster.

"Good God," she said evenly as she tried to make sense of the scribble. Some of the details had been crossed out and written over. Then, "Good God," more urgently, her eyes wide and startled. The third time, she was screeching "Good God!"

She knew who had murdered Donald Seaton and she needed to act quickly if she was to prevent another death.

Barbara Bellamy was curled up beneath the staircase, her mouth sagging open in her unconsciousness. Her neck gurgled. What else had the woman acquired from Donald Seaton's wallet?

Timbers crawled, carefully, thinking about each step, to the back of the shop's counter. When she scratched her shin on the upturned tray of bodices, she sat and rubbed it, holding back childish tears. Then, like an uncertain toddler, she climbed up the side of the counter until she was on her knees and able to reach the telephone.

"You won't find Ned in here, Timbers m'dear," said the North Country officer. "I've heard that he's gone for good. He don't work here anymore, someone was saying. Gone off on his bike, I reckon. Yes, you could try his home number but the word is he's properly gone. Can I help you, Pet?"

She asked for Inspector Hillier.

"Her neither, I'm afraid. Now, I do know exactly where she is. One of the fellows just phoned in. They've got her in a van full of desks and old wooden chairs. You won't be seeing Inspector Jennie for a week, I'd say, and the Lord knows the state she'll be in."

Timbers nursed the back of her head.

"Can I help, Timbers m'love?"

"I could try his home," she said.

Three miles away, someone was watching from my armchair as the telephone rang. My instructions had been clear – do not answer the door, do not answer the phone, do not switch on any lights that can be seen from the streets or spotted beneath the front door. My little helper stared intensely at the telephone, believing that her concentration might force the ringing to stop.

In Barbara Bellamy's shop, Timbers dropped the telephone and called me an arsehole. "You'd be here quick enough if I was washing my girlie bits at the kitchen sink, Ned Machray. But put me under a bloody train or make me know a murderer and you're no-bloody-where. Think I'm daft, you do." She sat, dejected, on the floorboards and said 'bloody' again. She looked at the unconscious Bellamy and knew that the woman would warn the killer as soon as she woke. Allowing herself no second thoughts, Timbers pulled the telephone from the wall. (It took four tugs and three more 'bloodies'.) She crawled to gather Barbara's shoes. She trapped the high heels in the counter drawer and snapped them. She found three wooden clothes pegs in the drawer. She crept to the front door, carefully keeping low because people were already on the pavements, and pulled down the green baize blinds. She forced the pegs between the door and its frame.

Then, having collected Barbara's mac from the banister post, she left by the back door, locking the shop from the outside and taking the key with her.

At twenty past eight on a Saturday, The Nore Road was busy with pedestrians trudging to work, shopkeepers setting out their pavement displays, and the slow traffic stopping and starting. Some cyclists dodged between the buses and vans but so slowly that even the practised riders wobbled on their saddles. Holding Barbara's raincoat closed at the front, Timbers reached the kerb as the 37 double decker was pulling away. She jumped on the rubber platform and, realising that she hadn't the fare, started to climb to the top deck. But Owen from Cardiff followed her. She paused, turned, hoping that Owen would want to press past her. When he didn't, she pleaded, "Come on, Taffy. You can see me any night outside the Hoboken." She let the coat fall open. "You know I'll let you get your pennyworth." She wanted to say, you've done it a thousand times when it didn't matter to either of us. But now, when I need you to help me, you're no-bloody-where. "I need you to let me off paying."

"Can't, girl," he whispered. "Too many people watchin'."

Timbers gave way to her frustration. She mouthed off and kicked spitefully at the conductor's ankles.

Taffy didn't cry out. He rang the bell three times, bringing the bus to a halt. When he grabbed her shoulders, she pulled herself free of the raincoat. Timbers tried to slap him; he blocked with his forearm and, in the same movement, gripped her wrist. His other hand clutched the seat of her skirt so that he should have had a good hold of her knickers. Then he pulled tight, which should have bought her to her tiptoes so that he could hoist her off the bus. Except she was wearing no knickers. Timberdick yelped like a whipped puppy as the bus conductor's technique bared her bottom, surprisingly, and she leapt off the platform.

She deserved worse, the conductor said, and the passengers applauded.

Passers-by stopped to watch as Timbers sorted herself out. "Bloody liberty," she grumbled. "What's up with you!" she shouted at an old lady. "Bloody gawping while I pull my pants out of my bum!" (Pretending that she had some.)

People gasped at such rudeness, but cheered when the lady pro-

154

duced a rolled newspaper and slapped it across the tart's face.

Timbers ran off in tears. She dashed through a school playground, jaywalked a dual carriageway, crossing traffic lights when they were against her, and barged her way from the front of shops to the back. Now, she was so upset that even when people called out to her, she ran on without turning her head. When she got to the flats, three children chased her up the common stairs.

"What are you up to, Mrs?" asked the oldest, her socks down and her knee plastered with Germoline. "We can help you."

My door was locked and no-one answered.

"You want to use his key, Mrs. We could show you, if we think you're Mr Ned's friend."

The other two said that she looked like a friend.

Thirteen

Timberdick's Second Case

When Timbers opened the door to my flat, she felt she had been fighting the city for an hour and getting nowhere, and neither Jennie nor I were there to help. She had been thrown off a bus and scolded in the street. She had been unable to get past my front door without the help of children. Now, as she walked into my home, she expected more failure. Wise intuition had prompted her to dismiss the children.

A dumpy figure in old fashioned clothes raised herself from the armchair and stood, very plain, in the middle of the room.

"Good God," said Timbers.

"I knew you'd find a way in. But Ned's instructions were clear. I was to let no-one through the door."

"Good God, the lav-lady."

"Listen."

"I've no time to listen. Where is he?"

Mo Tucker chewed her lip.

"The man you saw me with on the dog night – the Man from Scurries – he's bad."

Mo knew this.

"He's put a young girl in danger. He wants to ruin her life with his dirty dreams but, worse, he's put her in the way of a killer."

When the younger woman said nothing, Timbers perched herself on the arm of the empty chair and offered a hand. "You sent the letter, didn't you? You wrote to Cyn's mother, warning her about this man and her daughter."

Mo said, "I saw him following her after you'd been shot at. I knew what he wanted."

"I need to know when you wrote it, Mo. This is important."

"I've told you. After I saw him following her."

"You can't have, Mo. If you posted it the next morning, it wouldn't have got there-"

"I put it through her door. I did it in the middle of the night. I wrote it in bed, then I got up. I've," she hesitated, worrying her lip. "I've caught him writing things on the Gentlemen's wall. I know-"

"Yes," said Timbers. "You know all there is to know."

"We must stop him. I said to Jack in the café, no good would come of his meeting you. But Jack said leave it to Ned."

"Yes. We need Ned to help us, don't we?" Timbers spoke as if she was trying to convince a child of common sense.

"But I mustn't tell you where he is."

Timbers looked at the dopey lav-lady and shook her head, bewildered. "God, girl, what's he doing with you?"

"He's doing nothing with me," Mo pleaded, tears suddenly in her eyes. "He's not that sort of man. I did, once, get into his bed while he was wasn't here, hoping he'd find me, warm and naked."

"Oh – for buggers' sake-shut up!"

Mo lips trembled. "You shut up," she muttered.

Warm and naked, thought Timbers. Yes, she could see the fat old policeman liking that.

"He threw me out. The only time he's ever been cross with me. He's already got a lover, you know. And I know who it is and it's not you or me."

Before the revelation had sunk in, Timbers grabbed the girl's shoulders and shook her. "I've got to find him. If I don't someone's going to get killed. Soon. This morning. And if you know where he is you'll bloody tell me!" She drew back a hand and, without deciding to, slapped Mo forcefully across the face.

The girl screamed and dropped to her backside, more out of petulance than unsteadiness. Now, she would never tell.

Timbers picked her up and hit her again.

Then Timbers sat on the carpet and cried like Mo. "I've tried to do my best. Really, this has all been about Timberdick making sure that the baby and Cynful have a future. Even now, I know that poor Lucy's safety depends on me. And, just once, I want to get things right. Like, making up for the mess I've made of my life."

For an age it seemed that the world would go no further. Two girls sitting in tears on the floor. Both having lost things in their heads and neither wanting to carry on.

"I didn't know that Jennie and him were doing things," Timbers whispered.

"'S-not Jennie."

Timbers waited.

"'S-never been Jennie. Not even when everyone thought it."

Mo wiped her nose with her finger and sniffed noisily.

"Who is it?" asked Timbers, but not really wanting to know.

"'S-the girl who smacks his bottom." Her nose was running into her mouth and her hamster cheeks were swelling from Timbers' assaults.

"Has he told you anything about Inspector Jen?"

"Of course he has, but she wouldn't look at him, would she? Not in that way. Besides, Mr Ned's wasn't looking for a girlfriend, not in that way."

"The girl who does it'll be Slowly. Good God," she said, then she said nothing at all. What was Ned Machray doing with Betty 'Slowly' Barnes, she asked herself. She pictured the two fools together and wanted to chuckle inside; bile got in the way. And why had he told this toilet brush about it and not her?

"They don't make love," Mo explained. "He says it's nothing like that."

"No," said Timbers. "It would have to be nothing like that."

Mo saw that Timbers had gone very quiet and guessed the reasons why. "I shouldn't have told you." Two of her fingers tested the puffiness of her cheeks. "It was unkind of me."

Timbers was still weeping, not making a noise about it. "I'm exhausted," she explained. "I can't do any more."

"You've been wanting to hit me, ever since I was walking up Moore's Lane."

"Only 'cause you were scared of me."

"Wasn't."

"You were."

"Wasn't," the girl said more loudly. "It's because you all think I'm dopey, so I have to keep clear of you. Because you all think I'm easy to hit."

Timbers tried to laugh. "We both need him, don't we, for different reasons and he needs to get seen by Slowly at the end of every week."

"Oh, no. It's only two or three times ever, I think."

"Not likely, you daft duck. Slowly's too good at it to let it rest at that. She'd have made him one of her regulars by now. You know, girlie, I feel bloody cheated. I mean, he could have bloody said something. I mean, how many times have I let him look at me starkers? How many times – I mean, OK, it didn't mean anything – but how many times?" Timbers got to her feet like a baby giraffe, her bony limbs working awkwardly. "You stay here," she said and walked into my bedroom.

When Mo heard the Dogberry clock smash against the bedroom wall, she hurried to see what had happened.

"That'll teach him," Timbers said.

"Teach him what? He's done nothing to you."

"He should have bloody told me," Timbers said. "He could have done. Could have told me before other things happened last night."[8]

Mo was beginning to hate herself again. (She often did when things went wrong in the world.) "I've opened my mouth and you've got it all out of shape. You need to talk to him. You need to let him explain. Look, I can't tell you where he is, but I can get a message to him. I can tell him to meet you somewhere."

I was in the back of Jack's Café when he took the call. He said that I was changing into my engine driver's gear but I'd get to phone as quick as the dungarees would let me. (The Superintendent had said that I needed to arrive at my country rendezvous, looking like a long distance lorry driver. I spoke to Jack who said that all he had was a boiler suit. I said that would do and, when I'd got it half on, he said Harry Haw used to wear it when he was playing at his model railway layout. That's what he meant by 'engine driver's gear'.)

"God, you look silly," Timberdick said when she saw me outside

---

[8] Mrs McKinley repaired the clock in the back of her curiosity shop on the Nore Road. She pasted the fractured face and replaced the glass. She said it was much ado about nothing but I insisted it was much more than that. The clock was my favourite, I said

the Methodist doors. "You look so bloody silly. You walk silly and your head looks silly on your shoulders. I bet you look silly with your pants down, don't you? You got anything to tell me, Ned Machray?"

"I haven't got time for your pantomimes, Elizabeth."

"Oh, calling me Elizabeth now, are we? I suppose you call all your women by their real names when you want to be shot of them."

All my women? What was she talking about? "O.K. I've got to get out of the city. I've got a couple of hours, I reckon. No more than that. They want to send me on a police job, Timbers. I'm supposed to have left on the first train from the Town Station. As soon as they realise that I'm late, they'll get me picked up. You're right, I should have told you, but where could I have found you?"

"But you trusted Mo-in-the-Lavs, didn't you? Seems you count a whole lot of people before me."

"Timberdick, what are you talking about?"

She preferred to sulk. She mumbled "Ned, get me to the foreshore. I know who did the murder and it puts little Cynful in danger. The killer knows she's the one girl who can work it out."

I lifted my engine driver's hat and scratched the back of my head. "You've worked it out as well?"

"But I shouldn't have done. Look, we haven't time to talk."

"I'll get someone round to her house."

"No. She'll be at Lucy's. The beach hut, Ned. The garage on the water's edge."

"What for? I don't follow, Timbs."

"Oh, Ned! For God's sake help me. God, you don't know how much I want to slap your fat face, right now. But I haven't got the time to do it properly. And, bloody believe me, it needs doing properly."

I asked what she meant.

"We have to get to Lucy quickly. You said that she keeps the sportscar in one of the old railway huts. Come on, Ned, we've got to stop her."

The general-purpose vehicle that morning was an A35 van. Painted blue and white with a blue beacon on top, it looked like something silly from toy town. More so when the emergency bell rang because the clanging was three times as loud as the little motorcar deserved.

"The foreshore!" exclaimed Percy Poulton as we stood in the road outside the Methodist Rooms. "That's way off our beat. The skipper won't allow it."

"You leave Sergeant Rushton to me." I gave him no choice. I opened the back doors of the van and, holding her small square hips, I hoisted Timberdick inside.

"Come in with me," she said.

"I'll sit in the front."

"No. Come in with me."

I tossed the green monkey hat ahead of me and climbed in after it. There was no room and I was too fat so I had to lean across six roadside lamps with stale paraffin inside.

"God, I can just picture it," she said. "You and her." But I had no idea what she was talking about. "You must look ridiculous. A proper fool."

"Please, what are you going on about, Timbers?"

"I want you to tell me! I want to hear it from you!"

I couldn't understand how she had found out. I had always intended to tell her, of course, but the time had to be right. I took hold of her little cold hand. "All right. Timbers, your mother died at the beginning of the year."

Her fingers twitched and she made a little noise at the back of her throat. But she could say nothing; I saw in her eyes that I had frozen her heart.

I had got it wrong. This wasn't the revelation she had been expecting from me. 'Sorry' was on my lips but it was too late to say it.

"You knew my mother," she accused quietly.

"Not really. I met her last year, just once."

"You knew where she was. I have been waiting on the pavements all these years, and you knew where she was?" Her voice carried no anger, only disbelief.

Percy shouted from the front, "Where are we going exactly?"

"The foreshore," I instructed. "And don't ring the bell." Percy protested but stuck the engine in gear and, with a deliberate jolt, set off for the harbour. I sat next to Timberdick in the dim light of the van. "I'm so sorry, love. It wasn't supposed to work out like this."

"Oh, how was it supposed to be? When were you both going to tell me? And when did you hear that she was dead? Before the funeral? Perhaps you thought it would be too distressing for me to know. Was that it, Ned?"

I shook my head. "I only heard about it last night. Your step-father came to the Volunteer and told me."

"I have a stepfather?" At last, a hint of sarcasm crept into her voice.

"Timbs, why do you think Lucy's in danger?"

"So you don't want to talk about my stepfather?"

"The back of a police van on the way to an arrest, Timbs. It's not the place is it?"

"Did you ask her to come and see me, Ned. I need to know. Did my mother say that she wouldn't come?"

"The time needed to be right," I said.

"Oh! For twenty years the time wasn't right. What that it?"

"No."

"And you knew?"

"Only at the end, Timbers. Timbers, what did you think I was going to tell you?"

"I thought you'd say about Slowly and you."

"Oh, God."

She shrugged and I said I was sorry again.

I said, "You think Lucy murdered Donald Seaton?"

She pouted.

"You think that she murdered Seaton at Willersley, then raced the sportscar to the terminus before the train arrived. Is that it? Is that what you've worked out? That the car was fast enough to give her an alibi?"

"Don't be stupid," she said, bumping into me as the A35 bounced along the back streets.

"Well, then. She was waiting for her father at the station."

"No. She didn't know that he was on the train. That's what Fred Leaper told me while he was pushing chocolate paste down my pants."

I didn't know about that episode. I looked at her round eyes and said, while I pictured Fred's antics, "Then one of the passengers did it. Lucy knows that one of the passengers had killed Seaton and she was the getaway."

"Ned. She didn't know Seaton had been murdered and there were no passengers, other than Seaton and Barbara Bellamy."

Percy switched on the beacon as he turned right at red traffic lights.

"We'll be there soon," Timbers said.

I said I was sorry again; then nobody spoke until we approached the beach.

"Christ, we're too late," Percy Poulton said quietly. An ambulance was parked on the concrete apron and as we clambered out of the van we saw the crew stretchering Lucy's body from the makeshift garage.

Joe Lamey buried his wife's face in his chest so that she wouldn't see their dead daughter. "It's all your fault," he said when he saw Timberdick. "I said you were interfering with her. I said it was unfair." He had the same restlessness that Timbers had recognised in the Railway Club. As he spoke, he pressed his wife closer and closer to him.

DC Furrows had turned up in the CID Anglia. "She's done herself in with exhaust fumes," he said, caring little. He was shivering. His hands were stuck in his raincoat pockets and his feet were trying to keep his blood moving. "She's been dead an hour at least, I'd say by the colour." Then his face winced, like a man who short sighted. "What are you doing here?" he asked.

I didn't answer.

Lamey was still going at Timbers. "This wouldn't have happened if you hadn't asked so many questions. It's your fault. All your fault, you skinny cow."

"Arrest him," she said seriously.

I looked at her, bewildered.

"Arrest him," she repeated.

I stepped forward and put a hand on Lamey's shoulder. "Mr Lamey, I am arresting you for the murder of Donald Seaton on the night of-"

"God, Machray, what are you doing! I'm the detective here." The CID man snatched my hand from Lamey's jacket. "Have you lost your senses?"

Full of purpose, I said to the prisoner. "Fred Leaper didn't know you were driving the train that night." It sounded good, but it was all I knew.

163

Timbers explained, "He was expecting the driver to take over his night duty but he wouldn't have considered the arrangement if he had known you were driving. You live locally and would have gone home."

"When did he tell you this?" Furrows asked, not knowing the awkwardness of his question. "Have you been questioning him?"

"I didn't know how important it was, when he told me. We were thinking about something else at the time." Timbers produced the scrap of paper. "But when I found out that Donald Seaton had bought Lucy's sports car, it all fell into place."

Timbers spoke to the mother. "Lucy had Donald Seaton's baby, didn't she? He arranged for her to go to a London hospital and while she was there, he bought the car from a garage in Chiswick."

"Not a hospital," said the mother quietly. "Just a friend. He had a friend who looked after her."

"On the night of the railway accident, she wasn't waiting for her father. She didn't know that he was driving the train. She had driven down to the station with the baby and was waiting for Seaton in the old railway carriages. Together, they were going to hand over the child to another woman. "Mr Lamey, you told me that you stayed in the car while Lucy went to look for Leaper. No, she was going to check that her baby was all right in the old carriage. And while she was gone, you left the car and attacked the man who had ruined her life. On your way back to the car, you saw Barbara Bellamy looking inside. She'd know that the car was empty. So, you told me that you were slumped down in the dark. But, you had no need to tell me that. Barbara has never mentioned the empty car."

Lucy's mother cried aloud. Timbers thought, 'My God, the little baby is part of this family and I've torn them apart. His grandfather's going to gaol (if they don't hang him). One day he'll learn that his mother killed herself. He'll grow up with his grandma, a broken woman without wages.' She compared that picture with the comfortable life he would lose. The nice colours and plenty of space in Susannah Thompson's house.

"Cow!" spat Lamey. The abuse was so much in keeping with Timbers' own thoughts about herself that she made no attempt to move out of his way. Furrows and I stopped the livid father from reaching her.

"Lucy didn't kill herself because of the baby. She killed herself when she guessed that her father was a murderer. She couldn't stand the bad blood in her veins."

I had to push Lamey against the side of the van. "I don't think we'll fit him in here," I said. "Can we put him in the back of your Anglia?"

"Don't get bloody smart with me, Machray," Forrows said and reminded me that he was the detective. "We don't let pavement pounders nick murderers. Not on this Division."

PC Poulton was on the radio, asking for a Sergeant. It took some minutes to get Lamey in the back of the Ford. We shackled him to Poulton. When I looked for Timberdick, she was sitting with Mrs Lamey a hundred yards away on a tar painted bollard. They were looking across the harbour. Carefully, I walked up behind them. "You'll need to go to the station, Timbers. You'll need to explain it."

"Explain it to me," said the woman. "Don't I deserve to hear it first?"

"You know most of it, I think." Timbers spoke quietly and as kindly as one can say these sorts of things. "Barbara Bellamy told me that Donald asked her to look after the baby because the mother wasn't ready."

Mrs Lamey said without taking her eyes off her the sea, "His name is James."

"I thought she was talking about another woman, but she was talking about Lucy. Barbara was careful and even lived with James in the shop, so that her neighbours at home wouldn't notice him. But on the day Donald was murdered the baby was with his true mother for the last time. I think, she had agreed to meet Donald and the other woman in the old railway carriages. I think your husband swapped duties when he saw Donald Seaton getting on the train. I think it was that late. He had wanted to kill Seaton for a long time, I'm sure, but he didn't know how to do it. Not until he saw him sitting alone on the grass bank after the crash. Then, he took his chance."

The ambulance was driving away and the Anglia followed. "Sergeant Rushton's on his way with a WPC." I explained that they wouldn't let me drive the A35.

"They'll take you down to the station," said Timbers.

"Or home."

"Or home, Mrs Lamey, if you want."

When Timbers and I were left on the foreshore, I asked, "What happened to the baby?"

We were looking at the dark water, full of secrets. Two days before, everything had been clear in Timbers' mind. But now she had pricked her dream of being close to the child. And even if he ended up as Glenys Seaton's new family, he would have to endure an eccentric mother and Goodladies' dirtiest tart for an aunt.

But Susannah Thompson had no right to the Timbers' Train Baby. She was one of his father's many mistresses. Nothing more.

"We don't do things because they're right, these days," Timbers said. "We do things because we want nice homes. A good start in life means clothes and schools and holidays. It doesn't mean having grandmas and grandpas that you know. It's sick, Ned. We're like bees feeding on a pot of jam when we don't need to. And it's that sickliness that we're passing on to kids. We're telling them, life doesn't have to be good; it just has to taste good."

I asked what that had to do with her little baby.

"Everything, it seems. In the end, that's all there is to think about."

"So, where is he?"

"What did your man Kipling say? Power without responsibility? So, if I get it all wrong, it's not my fault. God, I wish it was like that."

"Where is he, my love?"

She waited for a couple seconds and let the water lap against the old weed-laden breaker.

"I don't think we'll ever know," she said.

Timberdick's First Case

Malcolm Noble
Matador Paperback (ISBN 1-904744-33-8)

Timberdick worked the pavements of Goodladies Road where the men had bad ideas and the women should have known better. When the local CID loses interest in the murder of a young prostitute, Timbers takes the case on. It's 1963 and Timberdick's First Case challenges more than her detective skills. "Real people are murdered by their family and friends," she is told by one of the girls. "We get killed by everyone else."

Timberdick's First Case is available from your local bookshop, Amazon.co.uk or Troubador (0116 255 9312; www.troubador.co.uk/bookshop)